Next Door To A Star

By Krysten Lindsay Hager

Next Door To A Star

Copyright © 2015 by Krysten Lindsay Hager.
All rights reserved.
First Print Edition: September 2015

Limitless Publishing, LLC
Kailua, HI 96734
www.limitlesspublishing.com

Formatting: Limitless Publishing

ISBN-13: 978-1-68058-269-7
ISBN-10: 1-68058-269-0

No part of this book may be reproduced, scanned, or distributed in any printed or electronic form without permission. Please do not participate in or encourage piracy of copyrighted materials in violation of the author's rights. Thank you for respecting the hard work of this author.

This is a work of fiction. Names, characters, places, and incidents either are the product of the author's imagination or are used fictitiously, and any resemblance to locales, events, business establishments, or actual persons—living or dead—is entirely coincidental.

Dedication

In loving memory to my father, Bruce, who supported me along my writing journey and always had faith in me. The best storyteller, supporter, and father anyone could ask for.

Chapter One

The school year should end right after spring break, because all anyone can focus on is summer vacation. You can't learn anything new, because all you can think about is all the fun stuff you're going to do once you don't have to get up at the butt crack of dawn. Summer always seems full of possibilities. Nothing exciting ever happens during the school year, but maybe, during summer vacation, you could run into a hot celebrity and he'd decide to put you in his next music video. Okay, it wasn't like I knew anybody that happened to, but my grandparents did live next door to a former TV star, Simone Hendrickson, and Simone was discovered in an ice cream parlor one summer. Of course, she lived in L.A. at the time and was already doing plays and commercials, so the guy who discovered her had already seen her perform. But hey, it was summer, she got discovered, and that was all that mattered.

Amazing stuff didn't happen to me. You know what happened to me last summer? I stepped on a bee and had to go to the emergency room. They're not going to make an *E! True Hollywood Story* out of my life. I didn't go on exotic vacations—like today, I was being dragged along with my parents to my cousin's graduation party. Most people waited until at least the end of May before having a grad party, but Charisma was having hers early because she was leaving on a trip to Spain. I was dreading this party because I didn't want to listen to everybody talk about how smart and talented Charisma was—making me feel like a blob in comparison—but my mom RSVP'd even though I said I'd rather die than go. My death threats meant nothing. But still, for some strange reason, I had a feeling this summer was going to be different.

We pulled up to Charisma's house, and I lagged behind my parents as we went to the backyard. My grandparents were already there sitting by the pool.

"Too bad Hadley didn't bring her bathing suit," Grandma Daniels said to my mom.

I had seen the whole "bring your swimsuit" thing on the invitation, but there was no way I was putting on a bathing suit and getting into a pool in front of people. And thank goodness I didn't, because it was a total high school party. When my cousin Donny graduated, he had, like, fifty old people there and only three of his friends, but this was a total teenager party, and there was a big difference between me, a ninth grader, and a bunch of seniors. Right now, sitting at the pool, the gap felt even bigger as I watched Charisma and her friends looking like models.

When I left the house this morning, I thought I looked good in my white and pink striped Forever

21 shorts and my paint splashed t-shirt. It was the cutest thing I owned, but I might as well have been wearing Osh Gosh overalls since I was surrounded by senior girls wearing bikinis. And not even the regular kind, but the ones with cutouts on the sides that had the metal things holding them together. I was way too short and skinny to wear something like that.

"Hadley, Charisma has some old suits if you want to try one on," Aunt Shelly said as she passed a cheese and cracker tray around.

"No, I'm fine. Thanks, though," I said.

No way was I getting in a bathing suit around all these high school girls who looked like goddesses. I'd like to think I looked at least my age, but I couldn't forget the first time I walked into my history class and the teacher told me the eighth grade class was in the other wing of the school.

I sat on my patio chair and watched one girl getting out of the pool. It seemed like fifty guys offered her a towel. She was tan with dark hair, super exotic, and pretty much the complete opposite of pale, dishwater blonde, short little me. Even without any makeup and her wet hair plastered to her face, the guys were drooling over her. There was also a couple who were completely making out on the side of the pool, right in front of my grandparents.

Aunt Shelly announced the food was ready, so we went inside. I noticed most of girls stayed by the pool. A few walked in and stole a grape out of the watermelon fruit basket, but none of them got a plate. Meanwhile, the guys were piling their paper plates full of baked beans, ham, potato salad, and whatever else they could fit on there. I always felt self-conscious about eating in front of people who were older than me—not adults, but teenagers.

Aunt Shelly told me to go sit with Charisma and her friends and walked me over to where the girls were sitting.

"This is Charisma's cousin Hadley," Aunt Shelly said. The other girls barely looked up.

"Are you guys all seniors?" I asked the girl sitting next to me

"Yeah," she said. "Charisma, can you hand me another Diet Coke?"

"Seriously, Kiely? It's been, like, four seconds since your last one," Charisma said laughing.

"Can I get one too?" I asked.

"So what are we going to do tonight, you guys?" Charisma asked. "Scott said we could go to his house."

"Um, can you pass me a Coke?" I asked again.

Charisma popped a grape in her mouth and adjusted her swimsuit. I saw her reach over to get a can of soda and I sighed in relief, but she popped the top and took a long drink.

"Charisma, can I get a soda too?" I asked louder.

She stared at me like it was the first time she had seen me all day. I swear, she wanted to ask when I had sat down with them. She glanced behind her into the cooler.

"Oh, sorry, Hadley. This is the last one. There's probably more in the kitchen if you want to go."

I got up and walked to the kitchen, but there were a bunch of senior guys right in front of where

Next Door To A Star

the drinks were on the counter. I turned and went back to where my grandparents and parents were sitting.

"Hadley, you have to come stay with us this summer," Grandpa said, reaching past me to get a napkin. "You could spend time at the beach and go out on the boat with us."

I shifted. He meant well, but I wasn't the kind of person who went to the beach a lot. I was more the type who sat in the shade with a book, in the privacy of my backyard.

"Why don't you come when school gets out?" he said, and then reminded me the actress Simone Hendrickson lived next door to them. Trust me, I hadn't forgotten. Oh, and did he mention how Simone used to be on the TV show *Duncan's Corner*? She was also in a TV movie, did a bunch of commercials, and was in a workout video…and was gorgeous with her round blue eyes and perfect blonde hair—not like my blah, dishwater-colored hair.

"You didn't get a chance to get to know her when you were there last summer," Grandma said. "It would be fun for you to have someone closer to your own age around for the summer."

Um, maybe she was forgetting the fact when she introduced me to Simone, Simone glanced at me, said, "Hey," and then told her mom she had to meet her friends at the beach. It wasn't like I expected her to hug me yelling, "Let's be best friends," but maybe she could have held back the yawn. I knew she used to be on some sitcom, but did she have to be so stuck up?

Simone used to play the youngest daughter, Abby, on *Duncan's Corner*. The show was pretty popular, but I hardly ever watched it because it came on the same time as *Video Request Countdown*, which was hosted by Jack Brogger, my favorite singer. I glanced around the pool. Why couldn't Charisma have guy friends like Jack? It seemed like real high school boys were nothing like the guys on TV. The real ones were scrawny with broken-out skin. If Jack were here, though—

"Hadley, do you want some cantaloupe? It's full of fiber. Helps you go to the bathroom," Grandma said, interrupting my Jack fantasy. I shook my head. It was probably better Jack wasn't here. He'd probably be flirting with the dark-haired girl or Charisma and break my heart.

My Aunt Faith was lying out on a pool chair looking bored. She had her legs out in the sun, but the rest of her was in the pool house so she wouldn't get sunburned.

"Hadley, I read in *InStyle* magazine a lot of celebrities vacation in Grand Haven," Faith said. "You should stay over. Who knows who you might see?"

"Seriously? Like who?"

"Well, a couple of the girls from *Duncan's Corner* came to visit Simone, and the actress Jerrica Adams came with her husband, and a bunch of singers, like Kevyn DeGarmo, Alfonso Carerra, and Jack Brogger—"

I sat up in my chair. "Seriously? Jack Brogger?" She nodded.

"My friend saw him out on a boat last year," she

said. "He rents a cottage."

"Cottage?" Grandma snorted. "The place where he stays is so huge that you wouldn't refer to it as a cottage by any means."

Faith nodded and said there was a big gate with a security guard out front.

"We tried driving past it, but you can't see much except the outline of that place—and it is huge," she said.

Time to rethink the whole spending the summer with the Grandparents thing. I looked over at my mom who said, "I'd be happy to get rid of you for the summer." Well, if Jack spent time in Grand Haven, then I had to visit my dad's family this summer.

I called my best friend, Lexi Irvin, as soon as I got home to tell her I'd be spending the summer in a place where Jack vacationed, and then I mentioned Simone.

"Oh my gosh, Hadley," Lexi said. "It would be amazing to live next door to a star over the summer."

"Yeah, but Simone probably hangs out in clubs or something. I doubt we'd hang out or be at the same places."

"Well, those beach towns are small, so I'm sure your paths would cross, especially with her being so close."

"True, but let's be honest. I'm not exactly the Simone Hendrickson of the ninth grade. I don't get invited to parties or have a closet full of designer clothes or—"

"Whatever, you do have a great best friend

though," she said.

"Yeah, well, at least I do for another week until you leave for Dallas."

"Don't remind me. Exactly five days," she said. "I can't believe I have to start over again as a sophomore. Everyone says it's so much harder to meet new people when you transfer in high school."

"I'm sure you'll meet a ton of new people," I said, and I meant that. Lexi was funny, friendly, outgoing, and everything you'd want in a best friend. I was more worried about how I was going to handle starting over on my own. I was way more of an introvert. I stared out the window as I thought about what life would be like without my best friend since the fourth grade. She was the kind of friend you could communicate with by exchanging glances.

"I can't believe you're really going," I said. "I mean, we talk or text every day. Who is going to like the pictures I post online of my breakfast?"

Lexi cracked up. "We're still going to talk and text every day, and I promise you—if you post a picture of your half-eaten oatmeal, then I will 'like' it."

I knew she believed that, but I also knew she'd meet new people and, well, forget about me.

"Listen, I gotta go and make sure my boxes are labeled for the move. I'll see ya tomorrow," she said hanging up.

The greatest thing about having a best friend was having someone always there for you—even when you make a fool of yourself—like when I tripped in front of my entire class while accepting my spelling bee trophy, although Lexi told me no one even noticed, and every dodgeball day in gym class pretty much made me an expert in humiliation, but we were always in it together. Now I was seeing the downside of having a best friend—being so exclusive with someone that you didn't have a lot of other people to turn to when your BFF moved away.

I sighed and reached in my desk for a piece of gum. My mom had warned me about hanging out with only one person all the time, but no one else got me the way Lexi did. Now, it felt like I was going to have to start all over trying to fit in with another group. Sure, I had other girls I talked to, but I didn't have a group. I didn't fit in with the super popular girls, I wasn't smart enough to hang out with the brains, and I wasn't athletic enough to be friends with the girls on the basketball team. At least going away for the summer meant I wouldn't have to sit home feeling sorry for myself.

Chapter Two

Lexi and I tried to spend as much time together as we could before moving day. On her last day, a bunch of girls who barely talked to her before were crying like they were losing their best friend. Isabella Bowman, the most popular girl in school, even asked Lexi to sit with her at lunch. Isabella always wore the latest stuff—she had a real Coach bag and not one of those knockoff ones, and all the other girls wanted to be her friend. If Isabella sat with you at lunch, then you were somebody, but if Isabella didn't know who you were, then nobody else did either…and they didn't care. Lexi and I used to talk about how great it would be to sit at Isabella's lunch table, but today Lexi didn't even ask me to sit next to her. I sort of followed behind them. My best friend's last day of school and I had to ask people to move over to squeeze in at the table. I guess I understood why she forgot about me, but I never would have done that to her.

I went over to her house after school to say goodbye and there were over thirty people there.

"Lexi, I'm really going to—"

"Just a sec—" she said putting up her hand. She turned and hugged a girl from our algebra class who I barely remembered her speaking to. "I will miss you soooo much, Kylie!"

As soon as Kylie moved away, I went to hug Lexi, but another girl, this one from our health class, beat me to it.

"Lexi! I cannot believe you're leaving me," she said, and a bunch of others crowded in. I stood back waiting until they were done so I could have a moment alone with Lexi.

"Okay ladies, Lexi has to get to bed early because we are hitting the road super early and she needs her beauty rest," Mr. Irvin, Lexi's father, said. "You can all text and e-mail later."

"Wait, Lex, we didn't get to talk," I said.

"Yeah, I know, sorry. Things got so crazy, but I will call you as soon as we get to Dallas. Maybe even if I get some time when we stop for the night," she said, hugging me. "I gotta go, my dad wants us up at four a.m. He's crazy. This isn't goodbye anyway, it's see ya when I see ya, 'kay?"

She smiled and I tried to smile back, but my eyes were filling with tears.

***

The next few days were hard. Lexi had been my lab partner in science, so once she was gone,

Mr. Jeffries, our teacher, had me work with Isabella and her lab partner, A.J. A.J. did all the work, so Isabella and I talked. It seemed like we had a lot in common, so, stupid me, I invited Isabella to come over. I hoped she'd see I was an okay person and want to hang out with me. Isabella told me she had to watch her sister after school while her dad was working, but she was nice about it. However, Isabella's best friend, Brittany Buchanan, was talking loudly in the gym locker room so that I would hear her.

"Did you guys honestly think someone like Isabella would want to hang out with a loser? Izzy just learned her lab partner's name and the girl has gone to school with us since sixth grade. How pathetic," Brittany said, flipping her frizzy red ponytail.

I shut down. I grabbed my bag and walked out of the locker room. I told Coach Jeffers I wasn't feeling well and he gave me a pass to see the school nurse.

"Do you want me to call your mom and have her pick you up?" the nurse asked.

Mom had already lectured me on how the school might hold me back if I missed any more days. Then I'd be stuck in ninth grade for another year, and even then all the other girls would still have bigger chests than me.

"I don't think I need to go home," I said. "Can I stay here a little longer?"

Nurse Cohen let me stay in her office during lunch and she even brought me some crackers. I had been eating lunch in the bathroom ever since Lexi moved. I felt awkward asking people to sit at their lunch table—everyone already had their groups or their best friend, and now that mine was gone, I was alone and looked desperate. I decided I'd rather eat a peanut butter sandwich next to a toilet than have to beg somebody to let me sit with them.

***

My mother met me at the door when I got home. I got bad vibes from the way her lips were set in a straight line.

"Hadley Alana Daniels, the school nurse called and said you've been in her office twice this week," she said.

"I didn't feel good." Great, did the school monitor how many times I went to the bathroom too?

"Is everything okay at school?" she asked.

I didn't want her to know I didn't have anyone to eat lunch with, so I nodded.

"Is it because Lexi's gone? Huh?" She put her hand on my shoulder. "What's going on?"

I pulled away. "I'm fine."

All I needed was my mother calling the school about Brittany. I didn't get why Brittany had turned on me during gym. She never seemed to have a problem with me before. I wondered if she thought I was trying to get between her and Isabella. Some girls could be weird like that and had to be the one everyone liked the best.

My dad came home from work, and naturally my mother had to tell him I was in the nurse's office…again.

"What's going on, Hadley?" he asked when my mom went upstairs.

I shrugged. "Nothing. Some girl was kinda rude

to me in gym and I needed to get away."

"Rude? What did she say?"

"I mean...nothing to my face. She didn't like that I asked her best friend to hang out."

"She's jealous," he said, waving the whole thing off. "Ignore it." Then he went into a speech on how these were the "best years of your life, so you better enjoy 'em."

Great, so it was only going to get worse? I didn't know if I could take it. I tried to explain it was hard to find a group to hang out with now that Lexi had moved, but my dad wasn't getting it. He didn't understand why you couldn't hang out with everyone. Then he told me to invite a friend over, because "they'd like you if they got to know you."

Then, a few days later, a new girl named Jennifer Yamaguchi came to our school. Mrs. Dultrieve had her sit next to me and asked me to show Jen around. I was feeling pretty positive to have someone new to hang out with. I showed her how to order her lunch on the computer in the cafeteria, and I took her to the library because I went there sometimes while everybody else went outside.

"The librarians don't care if you eat in the magazine section as long as you don't get crumbs all over." I pulled out my sandwich and my Jack Brogger bear keychain fell out.

"Are you a Brogger too?" she asked, taking her Jack keychain out.

"Yes! I have the bigger bear too. I ordered from the website and he has a little concert t-shirt on."

"I want one of those so bad," she said. "I've seen him in concert twice."

"Jack's my favorite singer," I said.

"Mine too. No one else at my old school was that into him. They like that stupid boy band from the U.K. Not one of those guys is anywhere near as cute as Jack," she said.

We watched Jack videos on my phone until the bell rang.

***

The next day, Jen sat with Isabella and her friends at lunch. I waited for her at her locker, but she never showed up. I had asked Jen to come over after school to hang out and watch *Video Request Countdown*, which was Jen's favorite show too. I sat in the family room and waited all afternoon for her. Mom thought Jen misunderstood and thought she was supposed to come over tomorrow instead. I nodded and went up to my room even though they were premiering Jack's new video at night. I didn't want my parents to see me cry.

***

When I got to school the next day, I saw Jen with Isabella and Brittany. I wanted to ask why she didn't come over, but I wasn't brave enough to go over there. I basically knew why anyway. I mean, why be friends with me when you could hang out with someone like Isabella? I bet the only reason Brittany wanted to hang out with her was because Jen's dad drove a BMW. Jen saw me standing there.

Our eyes locked for a minute, but then she started talking to someone else. I'd show them all when I got to hang out with Simone Hendrickson for the summer.

After school, I missed the bus and decided to walk home instead of calling for a ride. I had walked home before and it was no big deal, but today Brittany decided to follow me home. Her house wasn't even near mine, but she stayed in step with me every inch of the way. I held my bag tightly to my chest.

"Running home to play with your bear?" she asked. Oh my—Jen told her about that? How embarrassing. Why did I tell her about that?

Brittany's breath smelled like tuna fish and feet as it pressed against my neck. I pretended not to hear her and kept walking. I could see my house coming up and I broke into a run. I didn't stop until I got into my bedroom. I curled up on the bed, and my heart was pounding as I rested Jack the bear's head on my chest. I stayed there until my mother called me for dinner.

Chapter Three

The next few days were even worse. Jennifer had told Isabella and Brittany about how I wanted to go to Grand Haven to see Jack and made me sound like a weirdo stalker. So embarrassing. Isabella didn't say anything, but Brittany wouldn't let it go and she pretended to cough the word, "loser," when I walked past her in homeroom. To make matters worse, Mrs. Dultrieve heard Brittany call me a "loser" and made her apologize to me in front of the whole class. I wanted to die. I thought I might get my wish since Brittany seemed like she might murder me.

"Hadley, I'm sorry I said you have no friends and the only person who would ever be your friend is a bear because you're such a loser," Brittany said. I sank down in my seat. I thought Mrs. Dultrieve would see through her fake apology, but sometimes it felt like even the teachers were on the side of the popular people.

"See, not so hard," Mrs. Dultrieve said. "Now what do you say, Hadley?"

"It's okay," I said.

"You'll have to speak up. We can't hear you," she said.

"It's okay."

"Open your mouth wider, dear."

"It's okay." It came out loud and the whole class laughed.

I couldn't wait until school ended. Everything would be all right on June third—the last day of school. No more Brittany stepping on the back of my shoe as I walked down the hall or people telling me "this seat is saved" when I asked if I could sit with them. As soon as this year ended, I would be free until September. Or so I thought.

***

At night, I sat down to dinner with my parents. I was taking a bite of my dinner when my mom dropped a bombshell.

"Hadley, Dad and I have been talking, and we think you should go away to the school's camp this summer."

Camp? No way, they could not do this to me. I was supposed to spend my summer looking for Jack Brogger in Grand Haven, not going to some stupid camp for losers.

"That camp is more for the middle schoolers. High school kids can train to be counselors there, but you can't apply for that unless you've gone to the camp before, and I haven't," I said.

"That's not what we're getting at. We think it would do you some good to socialize more this summer."

"But you already said I could go to Grand Haven," I said.

"Yes, but you've had a hard time since Lexi moved, and this would be a great way for you to get to know some of your classmates better, and I bet there will be some new people there," Mom said as Dad handed me the crappy camp flyer my stupid school had sent everyone.

"There's swimming, hiking, painting—"

"I don't like to do any of those things." I interrupted my dad.

"You like to paint," he said. "Take your hair out of your mouth, Hadley. It's a disgusting habit."

"You can't make me go. I don't even know how to swim," I said. "I'll drown and die."

My mother reminded me I did know how to swim, so I reminded her of how I almost drowned in Mr. Stevens' pool six years ago. Mom said she'd write me a note so I wouldn't have to swim and told me losing one water-wing didn't count as drowning.

"Mom, I went underwater and I couldn't breathe."

"Oh, maybe for two seconds. There's plenty of other things you could do at camp," she said.

I almost started to cry right at the table. Summer was supposed to be my chance to get away. To get to know Simone and go somewhere I wasn't invisible and start all over. Maybe even be somebody else. To be anyone but who the people at school thought I was.

"Well, you can't spend your whole summer watching TV," Dad said.

Why not? He spent *his* summers in front of the

TV. There was no way I could go to some stupid camp with a bunch of people who didn't notice me now. I mean, I couldn't sleep without Jack the bear, and I couldn't imagine what would happen if I brought him with me. I had seen enough movies about camp to know there's always some kid who all the other campers make fun of for the whole summer. In the movies it was always some spoiled rich kid who was the target, but even then that kid was rich, so they didn't have too much to complain about.

"There's a girl my age next door to Grandma—"

"Yes, but your father and I thought this would give you an opportunity to get to know the kids around here. Now that Lexi is gone, you really need to branch out and meet some new people before sophomore year."

So my own mother thought I was a friendless loser and that I better make some friends now or else the rest of high school was going to stink. Fabulous. Well, maybe she shouldn't have sent me to some stupid private school with like, twenty kids in each class. How was I supposed to meet people when there was nobody to meet? And don't get me started on the boys. They were all short and talked about going to the toilet all the time. Sure, it would be great if I could spend all summer hanging out with people around here, but I knew I wasn't going to get to know anybody at camp. At least in Grand Haven I could have fun. Besides, maybe Simone and I would become friends.

She sighed. "Well, if you want to go to your grandparents'...I guess we did say it was all right.

Maybe you and the neighbor girl will hit it off."

Somehow I doubted we'd become best friends, but maybe we would hang out once in a while. And maybe Jack Brogger and I would be dating by the end of the summer too. Yeah, that was probably not gonna happen, but a girl could dream.

Chapter Four

I didn't even get to sleep in on the first day of summer vacation because Uncle Stu's SUV drove into the driveway at exactly eight o'clock. My eight-year-old cousin Clark, and Lily, who was almost two, were strapped in the middle seats, so I had to sit in the back next to all the suitcases. At least I wouldn't have Lily drooling on me, because she seemed to be getting spit everywhere. I had brought a book along, but it was hard to concentrate with Clark's video game, *Armageddon 5: The Final Bludgeoning*, beeping away. Somehow, despite the noise, I managed to fall asleep. As we pulled up in front of the house, I saw my grandparents and Aunt Faith waiting for us on the porch. Grandpa gave me a hug and helped Uncle Stu unpack the car. Aunt Maggie tried to give Lily to Grandma, but Lily was covered with spit and some red juice stuff she had spilled in the car, so Grandma handed her off to Aunt Faith.

"Aren't you a sticky baby?" Aunt Faith said as Lily blew spit bubbles at her. "Aw, so cute." Grandma pulled a tissue out of her sleeve to wipe

Next Door To A Star

Lily's hands. I was tired after sitting so long, but Grandma wanted us to go out to lunch so we all piled back into the SUV. We went to a restaurant and sat at a table overlooking the lake, and I split a pepperoni and mushroom pizza with Aunt Faith. I hadn't tried thin crust pizza before, and it tasted like a chewy cracker. Clark started whining about getting dessert. Grandma didn't think Lily and Clark needed any sugar, but she sighed and went along with it.

"Hadley, order something white in case you spill," Grandma said, pointing to my white Forever 21 sweatshirt.

"You can have whatever flavor you want," Aunt Faith said, rolling her eyes. I wasn't sure what to do, so I asked for a chocolate and vanilla twisty cone. Grandma handed me a bunch of napkins and told me not to drip.

After lunch, Uncle Stu, Aunt Maggie, and Grandpa played soccer with Clark and some neighbor kids. Clark had only been here for five hours and he had already made three new friends. Even Lily had found a toddler who was almost as sticky as she was. Meanwhile, I sat with Grandma, who kept telling Grandpa not to "be so rough" with the kids.

"Hadley, do you want me to take you over to see Simone?" Grandma asked. "I mentioned to her mother you were arriving today."

I did, but my outfit was wrinkled and my skin was super greasy after being in the car all afternoon.

"I'd rather meet her another day when I don't look like I spent hours riding in a car," I said. Of course, even if I took three hours to get ready and had Jennifer Lopez's stylist do my hair, I'd still look like a blob next to Simone.

Uncle Stu took us to the beach on Saturday. I played in the sand with Lily while Clark took off with his new friends. There were two girls who were lying out in the sun. One of the girls was Asian with long, dark hair and the other girl had curly blonde hair pulled back into a ponytail. They both had deep tans, halter top bikinis, and were reading *Teen Vogue* and *InTouch*. My dad wouldn't let me subscribe to any magazines because he thought they were a waste of money, so I had to buy them when he wasn't around.

I watched the dark-haired girl pull on a hoodie with "Juicy" on the back as they walked over to the snack stand and came back with what appeared to be a big red snowball in a cup.

"Hadley, do you want to come with me to get a snack or something to drink?" Uncle Stu asked. I followed him to the snack shack. I wanted the snowball thing, but when I ordered a sno-cone, the girl behind the counter told me they didn't have sno-cones and held up a red Popsicle instead. It wasn't what I wanted, but I started to reach for it until I saw some guy eating what I wanted.

"Wait, what's he having?" I asked.

"Oh, a Tropical Icy. What flavor do you want?" she asked.

"Red," I said.

"Cherry?" she asked, raising her eyebrow like I was stupid. Okay, so red wasn't a flavor, but I guess I didn't look too dumb since she was the genius

Next Door To A Star

who didn't realize a Tropical Icy was like a sno-cone. I went back to my beach towel and tried to figure out how to eat it. It came with a spoon, but the other girls had eaten it like an ice cream cone. I tried it and slurped all the color and flavor off. I watched the two girls reapplying their tanning oil and changing sides so they would tan even on both sides. Something about them made me wish I were invisible. They could have been models, and there I was with a toddler who was always covered in spit and my uncle with his attractive farmer's tan.

***

Clark and his friends went out on the lake the next day. Uncle Stu invited me to go along, but being trapped on a boat with a bunch of eight-year-old boys was not my idea of fun. I plugged in the TV, but my grandparents didn't have cable, so it was pointless. I had my laptop but the wi-fi in the house was weird and the internet kept going down.

I checked out the bookshelves, but all of the books were for adults and none of them seemed interesting. I guess I appeared pretty pathetic because Aunt Faith suggested we go downtown and check out the stores. Mom had given me some money so I bought a Cary McKissack book, a glitter glue pen, and some Gummi cola bottles.

"Don't tell Grandma I let you buy candy," Aunt Faith said. "She doesn't mind baked goods and ice cream, but she doesn't like us to eat candy for some reason."

I thought it was weird my aunt would worry

about hiding candy from her mother. Even my mom didn't care if I ate candy. We went to the juniors department next and found the perfect bathing suit. It was a purple tankini with silver paint splashed across it. It was much hotter than my plain blue suit. I took it into the dressing room along with a pair of jean shorts, some Capri pants, and a Juicy Couture t-shirt with a beach scene on it.

"How does the suit fit?" Aunt Faith asked through the door.

The suit definitely made me look older. It had a built-in bra, so it was like I *needed* a bra, instead of my old suit, which made me look like I needed an adult to help me cross the street. I opened the door and my aunt stepped inside the dressing room.

"You certainly look more mature," she said. "Are you going to get it?"

"Do I look stupid in it?" I didn't want to look like a little kid trying too hard.

"You look cute. Is it expensive?" she asked.

It was on sale and she told me to try on the other stuff while I was deciding. The jean shorts were a lot shorter than I expected, but all of my clothes were so boring. These were like something those girls on the beach would wear.

"What do you think?" I asked.

"A little short, but they're cute."

I was hoping for "hot," but I bought the swimsuit and shorts. Aunt Faith got me the t-shirt and Capri pants because they were the only things Grandma wouldn't freak out over. I also had to promise not to let Grandma see me in the bathing suit.

As soon as we got home, Grandma was waiting

Next Door To A Star

for us.

"I talked to Mrs. Hendrickson this afternoon and told her all about you. She said you should come over to see Simone," Grandma said.

I felt a cold trickle of sweat run down my side.

"Well, maybe tomorrow. I'm kind of tired after shopping, and I should probably wash my hair again before I meet someone—"

"Hadley, don't be silly. She said to drop over after lunch, so they are expecting you."

Well, this was what I had wanted, right? To meet and hopefully hang out with someone this summer? But part of me wished that someone wasn't a TV star who was intimidatingly pretty. The whole thing about hanging out with Simone had sounded like a good idea in my head, but the reality of it was pretty terrifying. Plus, Grandma was acting like Simone actually cared whether or not some nobody from Goodacre came over to meet her.

I went upstairs and put on my new jean shorts, but Grandma made me change so Mrs. Hendrickson wouldn't think I "always dressed so provocative." They were jean shorts, not bikini bottoms. Sheesh, but the Capri pants made my legs look better anyway.

"Now have fun and take the hair out of your mouth. You'll smell like a wet dog," she said.

I knocked on the door and Mrs. Hendrickson told me Simone was on the porch in back. I took a deep breath and walked to the back where Simone was sitting. Her long blonde hair was impossibly straight and shiny, and she looked like an adult in her tiny beige shorts and baby-blue halter top, while I couldn't have seemed younger or less cool if I tried. She was stretched out on a wicker couch talking on the phone. She didn't even look up at me, so I sat on a bench and waited for her to finish talking. She was in no hurry to get off the phone so I stared out the window.

"Asia, I'm so bored. There's nothing to do," she said, twirling her blonde hair. "I went for a walk today and I didn't see a single cute guy. Not one. I know," she said. "When are you coming back?"

Simone went on about how bored she was and how "life sucked." She hung up with her friend and then stared over at me, and I went into this whole thing about meeting her last summer, but she cut me off and said she was going to lay out in her backyard. I didn't know what I was supposed to do, so I followed her outside. She spread her towel out and rubbed some Chanel sunscreen on her face, arms, and legs. I had seen that lotion on the *Style Network* and I knew it cost a ton. I watched her lean back and put a towel over her face, while I sat there like an idiot. I couldn't believe she was only going to be a sophomore in the fall like me. She seemed more like an eighteen-year-old. Simone got bored after a while and said she was going down to the beach.

"Hey, do you have a swimsuit?" she asked. I nodded. "Go get it and we can hang on the beach, 'kay?"

Was that actually an invitation to hang out with her? I nodded and raced back to the house to change into my new bathing suit.

"Grandma, I'm going to the beach with Simone,"

I said as I walked to the door.

"Okay, have fun and take your phone with you," she said.

I took a deep breath as I headed over to Simone's. I felt like my whole life was about to change.

Chapter Five

I got to Simone's and she was sitting on the porch texting and waiting for me.

"Finally, I thought you died," she said. "Let's go."

Simone walked fast, and I had to almost run to keep up as I followed her to the beach. She stood on the sand for a minute, looking around for the best place for us. Then she went to the area right in front of the tan lifeguard with perfect hair. She looked up at him, flashed her perfect Colgate smile, and spread out her towel. Her towel said "Juicy Couture" on it, while mine had Hello Kitty on the front. I flipped it over to the plain side so I didn't look like such a kid.

I turned to ask her something and realized she was listening to music on her iPhone. I sat there unsure if I should be glad I was hanging out with someone or if I should try to get to know her.

"Simone?" I asked. She was moving her lips as she listened to the music, and even though her sunglasses were on, I could see her eyes were closed. I tapped her wrist and she sat straight up.

Next Door To A Star

"What's up?" she asked.

I lost all courage and said, "Do you want me to get you a soda from the concession stand?"

"Oh yeah, sure. That'd be great. Cherry Coke if they have it," she said as she went back to her reclining position and turned her music back up.

Well, at least she was talking to me, although she didn't offer me any money to get her drink. I got up and went to get her soda. As I waited in line, I noticed all the groups that were together on the beach. There wasn't one person who was there alone. I hoped Simone and I would hit it off so I didn't have to spend summer up in my room by myself. I would go broke with all the books I'd download, and eventually I'd run out of stuff to read. No, I was going to have to make an effort with Simone to become someone she wanted to hang out with.

I walked back to the towels with her soda.

"Thanks, doll," she said opening it. "We've been here ten whole minutes and that lifeguard hasn't even come over to talk to us."

"Well, he's working. There's probably a policy where they can't take their eyes off the water."

"Yeah, lame," she said. "But you're probably right. I'll have to catch him off duty, I guess. Want to go for a walk and see if there's anyone interesting over by the lighthouse?"

I nodded, and she told me we were okay to leave our towels there and I could stick my phone and sunscreen in her tote bag. As we walked, she stopped to take pics and post them on Instagram. I have only fifteen people on my account, and most are book bloggers who I don't know in person but liked to talk to. I showed Simone the photo I posted.

"Nice shot. I like to post pics for my fans, but ones that don't show exactly where I am in case anybody weird is checking my account," she said.

Here I was posting to my fifteen kinda/sorta friends and she was posting to fans.

"You must love being here year round," I said.

"It's okay. It gets a little boring in the winter."

"I'd imagine any place is boring after L.A."

"I guess." She stopped and looked out at the water. "Where are you from?"

"Goodacre," I said. "It's a half-hour north of Detroit."

"Is there stuff to do there?"

I doubted my sleepy town's movie theater and regular mall would impress someone who had gone to the People's Choice Awards.

"Sometimes my mom's work gets free tickets to games and we go see the Tigers or the Pistons. That's pretty fun."

"Some of the Pistons are pretty cute," she said.

"Once I got an autograph from one of them. It wasn't at one of the games. He was waiting in line to get coffee and my friend asked him. He signed our napkins," I said. Oh wow, I fangirled to someone who probably signed autographs all the time. How lame could I be?

"Did he, like, flirt with you or anything?" she asked, lowering her sunglasses.

"Well, he was twenty-eight."

She stood there staring and waiting for me to answer.

"Um, no…why? Do guys who are almost thirty flirt with you?" I asked.

"You'd be surprised. I've even been hit on by guys *in* their thirties," she said, rolling her round blue eyes.

"Gross."

"Hollywood is different." She shrugged and looked away. "Whatever. Do you want to walk all the way down to the end of the pier?"

"Sure. There are some guys who aren't ancient sitting down there," I said.

She smirked and opened her mouth to say something when her phone buzzed. "Instagram likes. I got fifty-eight likes so far. How about you?"

I looked down at my phone. One person had liked it and asked where I took the picture.

"Um, a few."

She nodded and then got up. "Gotta go to the bathroom. Be right back," she said.

I picked up the magazine she had been reading and noticed she had dog-eared a page with a soap star named Valeria Joseph. Valeria had straight blonde hair with bangs, unique-looking, squinty blue almond eyes, and shimmery tan skin. She was so flawless and gorgeous, I was surprised I hadn't heard of her before or seen her in another magazine or something. She had this knowing, confident little smirk, and in that one picture, she was everything I wanted to be and look like.

The interview was only about her hair and makeup, so I didn't learn anything about her other than the show she was on, but I took out my phone and texted myself all the names of the beauty products she listed as her faves.

"What are you doing?" Simone asked, sitting down.

"Nothing…texting my friend," I said, and then I looked up and realized Simone was on her phone and actually not talking to me at all, but chatting to her friend Asia.

"Connor sent me a text this morning," she said. "Oh my gosh, Asia, you know I would never like him if Morgan did. Don't even hint at that."

After twenty minutes, I decided to head back to Grandma's when it appeared Simone wasn't getting off the phone anytime soon. I would have stayed, but I had been in the hot sun for a while and was starting to feel a little sick and didn't want to end up sunburned. Simone did kind of wave when I left. Well, she put her hand up, sorta. I guess it counted as goodbye.

I walked in the house and Grandma asked if I had fun. I wasn't sure what to say, because if I said, "yes," and Simone never spoke to me again, I'd look stupid.

"It was okay, but Simone and I don't have a lot in common."

"Maybe you'd have more in common with Judd Lidstrom's granddaughter. I'll call and see if they can stop by later," she said. "Besides, you'll get to know Simone better as time goes on."

I nodded and wished I wasn't so pathetic my grandma had to set up "play dates" for me. Clark was only eight and he had made tons of friends on his own. He was never around, but I was always hanging around the house like a leech or something.

Next Door To A Star

Mr. Lidstrom came over with Charlotte later. Charlotte had a short, dark bob and huge brown eyes. Mr. Lidstrom kinda seemed more exciting and fun than Charlotte. Grandma told us to go outside, so Charlotte and I went for a walk on the beach.

"Where do you go to school?" she asked. "I go to Watson."

"I go to a private school in Goodacre," I said. "It's kinda near Detroit."

Charlotte was a mathlete and in some club called the "Future Scientists of America."

"I want to go to science camp this summer, but Grandpa wouldn't let me go because I have too many allergies and they're literally outside all the time there."

"Wanna walk on the pier?" I asked. "We can go down to the lighthouse."

"Sure. It's a good thing I put sunscreen on before I came over. It takes a while to soak in and I burn fast."

We walked down to the pier where some older girls were sitting with their boyfriends. I wanted to get out of there, but Charlotte was busy sticking her pasty feet in the water.

"Let's go back," I said, tugging her arm.

We walked back to the beach, but my back felt prickly from having those girls stare at us.

"Do you know why Simone stopped acting?" I asked.

"I dunno. She never bragged about being on TV or anything when she moved here. She was in my class because they held her back a year. She did get mad when they cast this other girl as the lead in the winter play last year," she said. "But she was right to be upset 'cause the other girl sucked."

Charlotte and I walked down to the ice cream stand. The cool girls I had seen on my first day at the beach were there. The one with curly blonde hair was drinking a soda. She was so tan and perfect-looking. I would have killed to be her. Then I realized Simone was sitting with them.

"Hadley, your nose looks like it's getting red," Charlotte said. "Put some sunscreen on."

Charlotte handed me the bottle. I tried to wave her away, but she wouldn't take no for an answer. She had put some lotion on her own nose and didn't even bother to rub it in. I tried to get her to blend it when I overheard someone from Simone's group make a comment about Char's sunblock-covered nose. I was super embarrassed and tried to steer Charlotte toward the boardwalk.

"Do you want to get a Tropical Icy?" she asked. "I've got some money."

The Icy containers were huge and the juice dripped out the ends so I went to get some napkins to wrap the bottom. I heard some girl say something about someone being "all gross and sticky," and I glanced up in case they were talking about me. The blonde girl I had seen the other day at the beach was standing with her boyfriend and they were looking at Charlotte. Charlotte had cherry juice running down her arms and on her chin, and I was embarrassed for her. Simone smirked at her and then walked over to me.

"Can I get a napkin?" Simone asked.

I handed her a stack of napkins and she pulled

one from the bunch.

"Um, I only needed one," she said. "I know how to handle a sno-cone."

I didn't know what else to do, so I laughed along with them.

"You guys know each other?" Simone asked, looking Charlotte over. I didn't want to say "yes," and be on the loser list all summer, so I shrugged. I had my back to Charlotte and I rolled my eyes.

Simone nodded. I glanced around, but Charlotte was gone. I felt horrible.

"Looking for sticky girl?" Simone raised her eyebrows.

"Um, I don't want to get in trouble for losing her," I said.

"Hey, we're going to grill hamburgers tonight at my house. Do you wanna come over later?"

"Sure, what time?" I asked.

"Around seven," she said over her shoulder as she walked away.

"Okay, see ya then."

I went to look for Charlotte but couldn't find her, so I went to tell Grandma I was going over to the Hendrickson's for dinner. Clark was always eating dinner at one of his friend's houses, so his empty chair was a constant reminder of what a friendless loser I was. At least for one night my chair would be the empty one. I put on my makeup and asked Aunt Faith to help me with my hair since I was useless with a curling iron. I didn't want to get there right at seven o'clock and look overeager, so I waited until five minutes after seven to leave.

Simone's mother seemed happy to see me. She

gave me a hamburger bun and told me to help myself. I got a hamburger and some chips and went over to where Simone was sitting with her friends. Simone was sitting in a big white lawn chair, but everyone else was seated on a big picnic blanket. There wasn't any room for me on the blanket, so I sat on the grass.

"Guys, this is Hadley. This is Lucas, Connor, oh, and Nick," she said, nodding at the boys and then pointed to the girls—the same two perfect-looking girls I had seen on the beach the other day. "And this is Morgan Kemp and Pilar Ito."

They all nodded, and I noticed Lucas, Connor, and Nick were the only ones who were eating hamburgers. Morgan and Pilar were both eating salads, and all Simone was having for dinner was a bottle of diet vanilla cola. She leaned back in her chair and pulled her tanned legs up. Simone had a baby-blue American Hotties hooded sweatshirt over her white tank top, and her hair was hanging over the back of the chair. Pilar's dark hair was pulled up into a high ponytail and it showed off her high cheekbones—like Valeria's. Pilar was wearing a denim mini skirt with Milan written all over it, and Morgan had her curly hair piled on top of her head and she was wearing a short t-shirt dress. Morgan was much curvier than the other two girls and Lucas kept staring at her.

"Did you try the macaroni salad?" Simone asked me. "It's super good."

"Pasta salad," Morgan said.

"Sorry, right. *Pasta* salad," Simone said. I shook my head.

Next Door To A Star

"It's so fattening with all the mayo," Morgan said. "Not like it'd matter to you."

She was staring at my legs, and I felt like a skeleton in shorts so I tucked my legs underneath me. Simone went on about how Morgan was so thin. Then Simone patted her own flat stomach as if she had a big belly and said she was the only one who had to watch her weight.

Nick looked over at me. "So where are you from, Hadley?" he asked. He had warm hazel eyes, and I almost lost my train of thought looking into them.

"Goodacre. It's near Detroit."

"Oh yeah, that's right near where the Pistons play, isn't it?" he asked smiling. He moved closer to where I was sitting. "You ever go to any games?"

I nodded. "Sometimes my mom's work gets tickets. She's a bigger fan than I am and she gets so into it—it's kind of funny sometimes." I felt my face get warm. They probably all went to games with friends, and here I was talking about hanging out with my mommy. So embarrassing.

"That's cool. I watch a lot of games with my dad," he said. "So you're into basketball?"

"I like to watch basketball and baseball. I suck at playing sports, but I get really into watching them. I guess that's lame," I said, feeling stupid.

"No, I'm the same way. I mean, I play baseball a little, but those guys—" He nodded over to where Lucas and Connor were sitting. "—They get on my case about being more into watching the game than going out and playing basketball or whatever with them."

"Yeah, the girls at my high school are all super

athletic, and I trip over my own feet if I change my shoe height." I felt my face get hot. "Seriously, why did I tell you that?"

He laughed. "I hear ya, I am about as coordinated as a newborn baby chick."

"That's still better than me."

"Did I mention that the chicken still has part of the egg shell on its head and it's running into the barn door?" he said. "Repeatedly?"

I cracked up. "That's quite the visual. I think I may have met my match."

The smile grew across his face. "It's nice to have someone with a great sense of humor around," he said. "No offense to the other girls, but it's sure nice to hear something other than them talking about each other or their lip gloss color or something."

I glanced over to make sure the girls couldn't hear him. Pilar and Simone were bent over looking at Pilar's phone screen, but Morgan was glaring in our direction. I was pretty sure she couldn't hear us, but she didn't seem happy to see him with me.

"Nick!" Morgan said. "Can you get me something to drink?"

"Uh, yeah. Sure," he said, getting up. "Do you want anything, Hadley?"

I shook my head and as soon as he went inside, Pilar and Morgan got up to go to the bathroom and Simone grabbed my wrist.

"I need another soda. Come with me," Simone said. I followed her to the picnic table and she picked up a brownie and started to eat.

"These are so good," she said with her mouth full. "Try one." I ate a brownie as Simone took another one. "Isn't Connor hot?" she asked.

"Is he your boyfriend?"

She scrunched up her nose. "Kinda. I guess. I thought he liked Pilar, but I guess he likes me now."

"Did Pilar say she was okay with him liking you now?"

Simone got defensive. "She said she was, why?"

"No reason. I just wondered." Simone seemed upset, so I went on saying Pilar didn't seem mad. I didn't know how anyone could tell how Pilar was feeling about anything, because she always had the same expression on her face. Pilar was pretty and exotic, but she always appeared like she had sucked on a lemon and smelled a wet dog.

"Does Nick have a girlfriend?" I asked, hoping I wasn't being too obvious.

"Not right now, but anyway, Connor wants me to go to a party this weekend. It's his cousin's party, but my mom would freak if I went 'cause he and Lucas are going to be seniors." She rolled her eyes. "Do you think it would be okay if I said I was going to your grandparents' house so I wouldn't get in trouble?"

"I guess it would be okay," I said. Simone gave me a big grin, and even her round blue eyes seemed to smile at me.

"Great, thanks. Have another brownie," she said. "They're gluten-free."

Morgan and Pilar came back and wanted to go to Lucas's house and take his dad's boat out.

"Wait, let me ask my mom," Simone said.

It was obvious I wasn't invited, so I stood there while Pilar twisted a strand of shiny black hair around her finger.

"You guys, she won't let me go," Simone said, walking over to us. "Do you wanna stay here and watch a movie instead?"

Morgan rolled her eyes and said they were going.

"Hadley, can you come with us?" Nick asked.

"Her name is Hayley, duh," Morgan said.

"Uh, no, it's Hadley. I had it right, didn't I?" he asked.

I nodded. "Yeah, but…I should probably stay with Simone."

"Okay, cool. So…see ya around then?" he asked.

I couldn't stop the stupid smile that was taking over my face.

"Yeah, I hope so." Did I sound too desperate?

"Good." The five of them left, but he turned around and winked at me. My heart felt like it shot up a whole story.

"Let's go inside," Simone said. She flopped across the couch in the family room while I sat on the floor.

"My mom never lets me do anything," she said, flinging a flowered pillow across the room. I put a cartoon in and Simone pulled her legs up and started picking at the silver nail polish on her toes. Her entertainment center had a bunch of DVDs marked with different episodes of the show Simone was on. There were like, a billion DVDs there, and I wondered why she had stopped acting.

"How long where you on *Duncan's Corner*?" I asked.

"Three seasons. Do you want some more chips?" She got up without waiting for me to answer.

"Is Nick a senior too?" I asked.

"Nope, a junior."

I stood up to leave when the movie ended, and Simone said she'd walk me back. We went through the backyard and she grabbed a bottle of regular Coke from the cooler.

"Ma, I'm walking Hadley home," she said.

We got to the backdoor and I wasn't sure what to do.

"Thanks for inviting me," I said.

"No problem. Now remember, if anybody asks, I'm going to be at your house on Saturday night, 'kay?"

"Right. See ya," I said and she waved without turning around. I wondered what it'd be like to be invited to a party like that.

Chapter Six

The next day, Aunt Maggie asked if I wanted to invite one of my friends to go to the movies. I couldn't invite Charlotte after I blew her off yesterday, and Simone had been to the Golden Globes before, so it wasn't like she was gonna want to hang out with my stupid cousin and his friends. Clark brought three of his friends and I wound up sitting next to Uncle Stu. The movie was dumb, but Josh Haven was in it and he was so sweet. Aunt Faith called him "the boy next door," but Aunt Maggie called him "cute, but kind of dim." We stopped for lunch on the way home, and the guys were acting out one of the fight scenes when Pilar, Morgan, and Simone walked into the restaurant. I wanted to die when Clark's friend Peter ran into Morgan's leg as she was sitting down.

"Ew, get it off me," she said as I slumped in my seat, hoping they wouldn't see me.

"Sorry," Peter said as he backed away from Morgan. She rolled her eyes.

"Uncle Stu, can we get the pizza to go?" I asked.

"What'd ya say, hon?" he asked. "Hey! Clark,

Next Door To A Star

put it down. Mister, I am gonna count to three and—" I asked again if we could leave, but by then the waitress had already brought our sodas so I was stuck there. Aunt Maggie went to get some more crayons so the boys could, "shut up and color." While I ate, I watched Pilar fix her hair in the reflection of the napkin holder. I swear she could make a mirror out of anything. I got up to use the restroom, and my hopes of not running into them were shot in the butt when I heard Simone and Pilar come into the bathroom while I was in one of the stalls.

"So is Lauren going to stay at your house?" Pilar asked.

"Yeah, my Mom's gonna pick her up from the airport," Simone said. "Remember, nobody's supposed to know she's coming. I only told you guys, okay?"

Were they talking about Lauren Gere who was on *Duncan's Corner* with her? I was dying to know, so I decided to come out of the stall. Simone and Pilar exchanged a look when they saw me.

"Hey, Hadley, what's up?" Simone asked, pulling out her lip gloss.

"Nothing. What's new with you?" She shrugged as she concentrated on applying her gloss. Pilar nudged her arm.

"We gotta go, but call me later, okay?" she said as Pilar pulled her out the door.

Great, so I wasn't worthy of hearing her big news. I was just good enough to cover her butt when she needed to sneak out. Whatever. I decided to forget about her...until I got home and realized I was dying to meet Lauren Gere. Simone probably couldn't say anything about it to me in front of Pilar because she had told her not to tell anyone. She didn't want to look like a hypocrite, right? So I called Simone and she told me to come over. Her mom was vacuuming under the couch cushions when I walked in.

"Are you guys having company?" I asked.

"Yeah, my friend Lauren is coming to visit soon, but I'm not supposed to tell too many people. She's super private," Simone said. "Want a soda?"

"Lauren Gere? From the show?"

"Yup. Do you want diet vanilla, cherry, or regular Coke? Cherry's my favorite," Simone said.

"Could I meet her?"

Simone stopped pouring the drinks. "Yeah, sure, but she recently broke up with her boyfriend, and she's afraid the magazines will come down here to find her. She was dating Stephen Harmon from *Fate's Wicked Twists* and they were on the cover of *Teen Vogue* together, and then he got a big movie role and dumped her for his co-star Tiarra Gregory. Anyway, he's kinda been in the tabloids a lot and there's been a lot of crap about the breakup in the magazines and stuff. She wants to hang out here and not worry about anything."

I promised not to say anything. We went into her room. Morgan called while I was there, but Simone told her she didn't feel like going out.

"Morgan, I don't feel like it. I know, but I have company right now. No, not Lauren, but—Morgan! Geez, let me talk! I have a headache and Hadley's here, so I can't leave right now. I'll call you tomorrow, okay?"

Simone tossed her cell phone onto her vanity. "She won't shut up about Lauren. It's so annoying. Let's go watch a movie or something." She got up without waiting for me.

Later, I walked past the Lidstrom's cottage on the way home, and Mr. Lidstrom was outside watering his yard. I felt so guilty when he waved to me. I wondered if Charlotte had said anything to him about what a jerk I was.

I walked into the house and Grandma and Grandpa were about to go to the store to pick up dinner, so I went along. While my grandparents were arguing over what to get to eat, I went to look at the makeup. I wasn't sure what I needed to get because my mom only wore blush and lipstick. Valeria said her favorite brand of mascara was Be Lashful and she "Couldn't live without Cover Girl blush and lip gloss." I picked up a tube of Be Lashful mascara, some blush, and a sheer pink lip gloss. I asked Grandpa if I could get some makeup and he nodded, but I don't think he was paying attention.

As soon as we got home, I went up to my room and dumped the makeup on my bed. I took out my favorite picture of Valeria and tried to copy what she had done with her makeup. I smeared the blush on, but my skin didn't glow like hers. I put the mascara on next, but I got it in my eye, which started to tear up and left watery tracks in my blush so I had to wash my face and start over. Now I knew why my mom didn't wear mascara. I tried it again and managed to keep the mascara out of my eyes. I put on the gloss and checked myself out in the mirror. A little better, but I didn't look a thing like Valeria. She must have used some other stuff she didn't mention, or I just wasn't as pretty as her. I wore my new makeup to dinner and Grandma noticed the lip gloss right away.

"Look at all that lipstick," she said. "Looks like you ran a lollipop across your mouth." Not the look I was going for at all.

"It looks nice," Aunt Faith said.

I leaned over and grabbed a piece of the cucumber she was chopping up for dinner. I asked her if she knew who Valeria Joseph was, but Aunt Faith hadn't heard of her.

"Is she a singer or an actress?" she asked.

"She's on a soap called *Charmed Lives*," I said.

"Your mother lets you watch those shows?" Grandma asked. "Those stories are a waste of time. Trash."

"I watch *You Only Live Once*," Maggie said. "The storyline's good right now—"

Grandma gave her a look and she got quiet.

"I don't watch the show, but I saw Valeria in a magazine."

Aunt Maggie said she might know who she was, so I showed her a picture.

"She looks like a Barbie doll," Aunt Maggie said as Aunt Faith glanced over her shoulder. If Faith had longer hair and wore a lot more makeup, she might look a little bit like Valeria. Grandpa came in the kitchen to get the barbecue sauce and saw my magazine.

"Hey, Chandler Ashton," he said.

Chandler Ashton was Valeria's character on the show. Grandma asked him how he knew her name and he shrugged.

"I must have seen her on a news program or something," he said. "Am I going to do the corn on the grill too?"

"Dad, do you watch *Charmed Lives*?" Aunt Maggie smirked.

"You know your mother doesn't approve of those types of shows," he said. "Hadley, do you want to set the table?"

I nodded, but I hated eating outside, because you get bugs in your face and you spend the whole time guarding your food. Clark was eating at his friend's house for dinner, so I was stuck sitting next to Lily, who was having toddler meat sticks for dinner. She kept waving her hands around and getting hot dog water on me. Then she dumped her toddler cup over my plate and little drops of juice got on my potato chips. Aunt Maggie took the cup away from her, but my chips still had red stuff all over them.

After dinner, Grandpa took us out on the boat. Aunt Faith stayed home because she gets seasick. I was nervous at first, but it was kind of fun when the boat hit choppy water. Grandma didn't find it fun at all and she kept telling Grandpa to slow down. My mascara was smeared under my eyes when I got back to the house.

"Weird question, but why does Charlotte live with her Grandpa? Where are her parents?" I asked Aunt Maggie as we walked inside.

"Her mom passed away two years ago from a rare blood disorder. Her parents got divorced a long time ago," she said. "I don't know if she sees her dad—"

"He was no good," Grandma interrupted. "Her mother was a saint to put up with him."

Maggie touched my arm. "Why don't you go over there with some cookies?" she said. "We're going to do boring grownup stuff tonight. You should hang out with your friend."

I figured even if Charlotte hated me, there's no way anyone would slam the door in my face if I had homemade cookies. So I took my chances and walked over and rang the doorbell.

"Those cookies look good," Mr. Lidstrom said when he answered the door. "Let's get a nice glass of milk to go with those."

Charlotte took a cookie without saying anything. They were watching *Entertainment Tonight*, so Mr. Lidstrom took the plate into the family room. Char sat back down on the couch. She was looking through old issues of gossip magazines and some issues of *Soap Opera Digest*. She didn't say anything, so I picked up one of the issues and started to flip through it.

"Here," she said, pushing something toward me. It was a picture of Jack Brogger.

"Thanks," I said, hoping the gesture meant she wasn't too mad at me anymore. "What's new?"

She shrugged and kept turning pages. Then she looked up. "Do you want to go downtown tomorrow and hang out at noon?"

"Yeah, I'd love that."

She nodded slowly. "Okay."

Uncle Stu sent me a text saying it was getting

late and Grandma wanted me home, so I got up to leave.

"See you tomorrow?" Char asked.

"Definitely."

Chapter Seven

Simone called me the next morning and asked me to come over. I knew I should go meet Char, but I didn't know if Simone would ever invite me over again. I mean, it wasn't like TV stars regularly called my house. Okay, so it wasn't like *anybody* called my house, so I couldn't tell Simone I was busy—especially when Lauren Gere was coming to town. Instead, I called Charlotte and told her I couldn't hang out today. She started to ask why, but I said my grandpa had to use the phone. I felt so crappy lying to her, but I figured she'd understand if she had the chance to hang out with Simone, wouldn't she?

Simone was sitting on her bed when I walked in her room. She was wearing a tiny orange t-shirt that showed off her tan stomach, designer jeans, and a pair of straw platform Steve Madden sandals. I had never seen anybody at Goodacre Academy wearing clothes like that. Brittany and Isabella would die if they saw me hanging out with somebody like Simone. I would have to get somebody to take a picture of us together before I left Grand Haven so I could show everyone back home I was friends with a TV star. I wasn't sure Simone considered me her friend, but still, she had invited me over.

"So guess what? *Major* news. Nick Jenkins e-mailed me about you," she said.

I sat down in a chair that was like a giant birdcage, and it swung out underneath me.

"I hate those chairs," she said as I almost fell out. "My mother has a thing for shabby chic. It's so weird. Promise me you'll never attempt to sit in that thing in front of Nick."

"Sorry, so what exactly did he say?" I asked. "Don't leave anything out. Not even one word he uttered."

"He wanted to know how long you were staying in town and if you had a boyfriend and…wait for it…if you had asked about him."

"What did *you* say?" I leaned so far forward that I almost tipped out of the stupid chair again.

"I played it totally cool. I said, 'She might have asked. I can't remember. I want to say she did ask about you, but it was such a crazy night.' Then he asked if I'd bring you along the next time we all go out together."

"Seriously? Are you for real?" Is this when she was going to ask if I'd come to the party with her so we could all hang out together?

"Yup. He said you were super funny and sweet and he definitely wanted to get to know you better. Do you want something to drink?" she asked.

I hated diet soda, but Simone always drank it, so I said I wanted a diet vanilla soda. She came back with two bottles, and I moved to sit on her bed because I kept bumping my head on the birdcage chair. She kicked off her gorgeous sandals and motioned toward my sneakers.

"I can't stand wearing shoes in the summer," she said.

"Me neither. I, um…couldn't find my sandals," I said. "So…anyway, is Nick going to be at that party tomorrow?"

"Oh yeah, he'll definitely be there," she said, and I held my breath as I waited for her to invite me to go with her.

"So, is it still okay if I say I'm at your house tomorrow?" she asked, leaning forward. I could smell her lime-scented body lotion. I didn't know what to say, so I nodded and she jumped up. "Great, let's go get some ice cream."

As I followed her out the door, I felt defeated. Like I had gotten so close, but still wasn't getting asked to hang out with the popular crowd. But Nick had asked about me, and that was something.

Simone wanted to go to the ice cream place where all the high school guys hung out, but there was hardly anybody in there when we walked in. She ordered a waffle cone with cookie dough ice cream, which was my favorite flavor too.

"Ew, there's nobody good here," she said, looking around for a table. She went back to the guy behind the counter. "Can I get this dipped in sprinkles?" she asked, leaning across the counter and smiling up at him.

He dipped her cone and told her it was on the house even though the sign said it cost a dollar for sprinkles.

Next Door To A Star

"Can I get a cup of water?" I asked.

"Yeah, but it's a dollar-fifty," he said.

I gave him the money even though I didn't see a price for teeny-tiny paper cups of water listed on the menu. Simone grabbed my arm and pulled me out of there.

"Let's go in here. They have the cutest accessories," she said, walking into a boutique. "Look at these palm tree earrings. So cute and they have two pairs if you want one too."

I told her my ears weren't pierced and she offered to pierce them for me.

"All you need is an ice cube, a bunch of towels, and—"

"It's okay," I said. "I'll think about it."

"Whatever. I'm getting a pair for Lauren. Oh, let's go to the drugstore next," she said. She walked in and headed straight for the magazine rack. I mentioned I had read about what makeup Valeria liked and her eyes got big.

"I love her," she said. "I did a commercial with her when I was ten and she was so sweet. I never miss *Charmed Lives*."

"I bought some of the stuff she said she uses, but I can't get the shimmery look she has," I said.

"Follow me," she said. She went to the makeup aisle, picked up a sample tube, and squeezed a tiny bit of shimmer stuff onto her hand. "I love this stuff. You can put it on your cheeks, eyes, and lips. Oh, you need to get some bronzer too."

"What's it for?"

"It makes you look tan."

I let her pick out some shimmer cream and

bronzer for me. We were going up to the counter when we ran into Charlotte and her grandpa. My stomach dropped. Simone went to get some gum, leaving us alone. Charlotte stared at the floor.

"I forgot I said I'd do something with Simone today," I said, talking way too fast. I sounded so guilty and slimy. "Can you come over on Saturday? I really want to hang out with you."

"Whatever." Charlotte shrugged.

"Hadley? C'mon." Simone was standing by the counter.

"So…see ya soon?" I asked and Charlotte nodded without looking at me.

I felt like the worst person ever, but Simone talked all the way back to her house. As I sat on her bed, I realized all I had wanted this summer was to make new friends, and I had finally stepped out of my comfort zone and done that, but I had also made a friend feel like crap and I didn't know if she believed my weak response. Life was so much easier when it was only me and Lexi…the same Lexi who swore we'd text every day and had messaged me a total of eight times since she moved. Could anyone be counted on?

"Hadley, you're not even paying attention," Simone said, tapping the shimmer tube against her palm. "See? You have to mix it all up and there are certain parts of your face which are supposed to be bronze, like your forehead, and other parts meant to be lighter and shimmery, like the tops of your cheekbones."

She pulled out a pink egg shaped sponge and started to apply it.

Next Door To A Star

"The pink shimmer stuff goes on your cheeks and on the crease of your eye, but the white shimmer goes on your forehead, part of your nose, and the brow bone. Got it?" she asked.

I nodded, but was totally confused. Did some girls instinctively know how to do stuff like this, or was it something you learned? And if so, where were they all learning this? I felt like there was some class I missed, like the time I was home sick when my class learned how to tell time on a clock. I swear ever since then, I have to mentally count to know what time it is—I can't automatically figure it out like the rest of the world can.

"Okay, bronzer is next," Simone said, taking a little brush and lining my eyes with dark plum eye shadow. "I always wear dark eyeliner to make myself look older. It makes my eyes look super blue. Now go like this," she said, sucking in her cheeks. "If you shade this part underneath your cheeks, it looks like you have noticeable cheekbones."

"Did you learn that from a makeup artist?" I asked.

She shrugged. "Don't remember. Do you want me to curl your eyelashes or do you want to do it yourself?"

I let her do it since I wasn't even sure what to do with the eyelash curler. I'd probably poke my eye out.

"I can't leave the house without curling my lashes," she said. She pinched my lid a little bit and my eyes started to water. "Okay, what do ya think?"

I picked up the mirror and I didn't look like

Valeria's twin, but Simone had given me noticeable cheekbones and my eyes were bigger somehow.

"It's amazing. I don't even look like myself."

She nodded. "Yeah, isn't it great?"

Later, Grandma noticed my new look as soon as I walked in the house.

"What's on your face?" she asked. I told her Simone did my makeup. "Her mother's got her hands full with her," she said.

Chapter Eight

I was trying to copy the makeup techniques Simone used on me when Charlotte came over the next day.

"You have a smudge on your face," Charlotte said, squinting at me.

"It's bronzer. It's supposed to make me look tan," I said.

"It makes you look dirty."

"Well, Simone wears it all the time." I rubbed my cheek.

"She's so tan she's almost orange. She's probably fake-baking to keep up with Morgan and Pilar. You know they're all going to get wrinkles and sun damage."

"Do you know that Nick guy she hangs out with?"

"Yeah, he's really sweet and cute," she said. "He went out with Morgan for a little bit. Like, for two days, or something. He's not like those two jerks he hangs out with—Connor and Lucas."

I filled her in on what Simone said

"Hadley, it sounds like he was asking her to

bring you to the party, but she used you for an alibi instead." Charlotte bit her lip.

"Well, I had already promised I'd cover for her before he asked, so…you know…no biggie."

"I dunno, I'd be sort of mad myself," she said. I thought it was weird that she wouldn't look at me.

Charlotte was right though—it might have been my only chance for Nick to ask me to hang out. He'd probably meet someone else at the party and forget all about me.

"Well, anyway, you probably wouldn't like him once you got to know him if he hangs out with that crowd, right? I mean, any guy who goes out with Morgan…" She shrugged and cleared her throat. "Anyway, look what I brought over for you. Remember when we were talking about books we loved back in the day? Well, I found my copy of *The Lion, the Witch, and the Wardrobe.*"

She handed it to me and she started looking through my books when an article I had printed out about Valeria fell out of one of my magazines.

"What's this? Are you getting your hair cut?" she asked.

"No. There's an interview of the actress who plays Chandler in it."

She glanced at the interview. "It's all about makeup and hair stuff. I didn't know she dyed her hair."

I got up. "She does? Where does it say she dyes it?"

"It says, 'Valeria goes for touchups every six weeks for her base color.'"

I felt dumb admitting I hadn't paid attention to

that. I told Char how Simone had done a commercial with Valeria once.

"Was she nice?" she asked.

"Yeah, Simone liked her, but don't you think it's weird Simone never talks about being on TV?"

"I dunno. Never thought about it. She told you about the commercial though," she said.

"Yeah, I guess. Hey, have you ever wanted to get your ears pierced?"

"No way. Why would I want to put holes in my body?" She stuck her tongue out.

"I don't know. It's kind of pretty." I shrugged. "I might let Simone pierce mine."

Charlotte almost fell off the bed laughing. "I hope you have a blood donor nearby," she said. "I wouldn't let her sharpen my pencil, much less poke a hole in my body."

"Whatever, I might do it."

"Well, good luck with that. Hey, do you want to go to the nature center with me and my grandpa tomorrow?"

I wasn't into science, and to be honest, it sounded boring, but Char said the place had a pretty view of the lake and she mentioned Conner, the guy Simone liked, had an older brother, Sam, who worked there.

"Is the brother cute?"

Charlotte made a face. "Please don't turn into one of them."

"One of who?"

"Never mind. Anyway, you'd probably think so. Sam's the kind of guy who knows he's cute, but he's always super nice to me when I go in there," she said. "I know it's not your kind of thing, but will you come?"

"Yeah, sure."

***

Simone called me the next morning. She wanted to come over to tell me about the party, but I had to tell her I was busy because I couldn't cancel with Charlotte again.

"Fine, whatever. Nick asked about you again. Anyway, call me when you get back," she said, hanging up before I could respond.

I had done the right thing, but that fear of Simone never calling me back again kept creeping into my mind. Plus, there was the whole fact she had news about Nick. I tried to ignore the feeling as I ate my breakfast and checked my phone for messages.

"Hadley, must you have that phone by you twenty-four seven?" Grandma asked.

"I sent a text to my best friend, Lexi, and I'm waiting for her to respond."

"Well, you can respond after you're done eating," she said, sliding my phone away from me. "The Lidstroms will be here any minute, and you don't want them waiting for you to finish your cereal."

On cue, the doorbell rang. Grandma sighed. "Fine, take a Pop Tart with you. You can't start the day on an empty stomach."

Aunt Faith let Charlotte in. Char took one look at my feet and said, "You better put on your Skechers or some hiking boots. Sandals aren't a good choice."

I changed my shoes and Mr. Lidstrom took us to the nature center, which was a big log cabin with stuff about leaves and animals in it. Charlotte was in heaven as we walked around. The center had a game where you put your hand in a bunch of different boxes with rubber doors over them and tried to figure out what was inside by touch.

"Are you going to try it?" Mr. Lidstrom asked me.

"I will put my hand in only after you've gotten *your* hand safely back and tell me what's inside."

He laughed, but Charlotte stuck her hand in each one without worrying she'd end up touching some big slimy thing. There was this kid's dad there who kept pretending something on the other end had eaten his hand off. It wasn't funny the first time he did it, and it was super annoying the twenty-third time he did it.

"Are you up for the hiking trails?" Charlotte asked. "They're fun because there are these steps built into the hill and we can take leaf and flower samples."

We walked over to the stairs and started to climb up. Mr. Lidstrom said he'd wait for us at the bottom.

I was glad I had changed my shoes because my feet would have been destroyed walking up that hill.

"Isn't this gorgeous?" Charlotte asked as she reached over to pick a couple of wildflowers. I nodded out of breath.

"Come on, we're almost near the top," she said.

"It'll all be worth it. Promise."

I followed her up the hill, and when we got to the top it was epic—you could see for miles—miles and miles of dark blue water. The lake looked gorgeous as it shimmered under the sunlight.

"See? Told ya it was worth it." She smiled.

I pulled out my phone to take pics and even Charlotte took a few of her own.

"Are you posting them on your page?" she asked.

I nodded. "With the hashtag 'best summer ever.' Are you ready to go back down?"

"Can we sit for a while?"

We sat on a bench crafted out of logs and looked out at the water.

"It's so peaceful here. I can't remember the last time I was someplace so quiet," I said.

Charlotte nodded. "I love it here. It's my favorite place. I came up here a lot after my mom died. You know, Grandpa can't climb the steps the way he used to and he doesn't like me coming up here by myself, so I'm really glad you were able to come with me today. It means a lot to me."

I smiled. "I'm glad I came too." It was kind of nice to be someplace where I wasn't worried about fitting in or how I looked or if I was being judged. It felt comfortable, like when I slipped on my favorite pair of yoga pants fresh from the dryer—the super worn out pair Mom wouldn't let me wear outside the house, but that I could never throw out.

We walked back down the hill and Charlotte got a couple of books from the gift shop. Her grandpa bought us both journals that had dried purple flowers on the cover.

I posted a picture of mine on my page and I got an instant reply from Simone asking if she could come over later. I wrote back:

Sure!

"Hadley, do you want to come over?" Charlotte asked.

"Char, her grandma will probably want her home," Mr. Lidstrom said. "Do you want to call and ask her?"

I didn't think Grandma would care when I got back, but Simone had asked if she could come over, and I really wanted to see her too.

"I should probably get back," I said, and they dropped me off at the house. I called Simone as soon as I got inside, but her mother said she was gone. Guess she wasn't sitting around waiting for me, but as long as she included me when everyone got to meet Lauren, then everything would be perfect and I'd know that I was fitting in with her group.

Chapter Nine

Simone didn't call me back that night or the next day. It rained all day so I couldn't go to the beach, and Charlotte had a stomachache so she couldn't come over. I went into the family room to plug the TV in, but Grandpa was already in there watching *Charmed Lives*.

"You *do* watch this show?" I asked.

"Do not let your grandmother know. She thinks I'm in here taking a nap," he said, looking nervously behind him. "Charlotte's grandfather got me into it last year."

I found out Grandpa didn't like Chandler's sister, and he thought Lance was Chandler and Madison's half-brother, so neither girl would end up dating him.

"See, Lance keeps talking about how he came to Orchard Valley to find his long lost sisters," Grandpa said. "That's gotta be Madison and Chandler."

"Maybe that's why they've never dated. I mean, Chandler's dated every other guy on the show, but not Lance."

Next Door To A Star

"Yup, those writers think they can pull one over on us," he said, nudging me. "Not likely."

We heard Grandma coming and he turned off the TV.

"What are you two up to?" she asked.

"Nothing, talking about this rain," Grandpa said. "Crazy, crazy weather we're having."

"Uh-huh," she said and walked out of the room.

As soon as she was gone, he turned the TV on. "Don't worry, I paused it first," he said. "We won't miss a second."

I smiled.

***

Simone hadn't called me by Monday, and Charlotte was still not feeling well, so I stayed inside again. Aunt Faith took me to the library after lunch and we were the only two people in there besides the librarian. There were two beat up chairs in the back, so Aunt Faith and I sat and read old copies of *InStyle* and *Life and Style* for a while. There was a whole article on summer jewelry, and it seemed like every teen celeb had dangly earrings on in the magazine.

"Faith, when did you get your ears pierced?" I asked.

"I don't remember. I think I was thirteen. Why?"

"I want to get mine done," I said.

"I'm surprised you don't have pierced ears already. Most girls your age who want them, have them. Have you asked your parents?"

"Mom thinks I'll get some weird infection or

something," I said. "But I'll take care of them, and they're my ears."

"What about your dad?" she asked.

I shrugged. "He doesn't care, but he thinks it's kind of stupid." Actually, what Dad had said was, "What kind of moron puts holes in their head?" Then my mom pointed out she had pierced ears and he shut up pretty quick.

I asked Grandma if I could get my ears pierced when I got home. I thought she'd freak out, but she was also surprised I didn't have them pierced already.

"Would you take me to get them done?" I asked. My parents couldn't object if Grandma was onboard with the idea.

"I will if your parents okay it," she said.

"They don't think I'm mature enough though. It's not fair," I said to Aunt Faith. "Everybody's got pierced ears but me. Even Lily has earrings."

"That's true, the little one does have them," Grandma said, and she and Aunt Faith exchanged a knowing look.

"So it's really important to you?" Aunt Faith asked.

I nodded. "I'm the only girl I know of in high school that doesn't have her ears pierced."

"Well, I was younger than you when I got mine done and it turned out okay for me, but you have to promise to take care of them and get it done by a doctor," she said.

She called a couple of doctor's offices, but none of them pierced ears.

"What about trying Slater's Jewelry Store?

They're reputable," Grandma said. "But I had no part in this if your parents ask."

***

Aunt Faith took me to the jewelry store the next morning and a woman named Michalina sat me down and showed me how to turn and clean the earring posts. Michalina asked if I had any questions about cleaning them, but all I wanted to know was if it would hurt.

"It might pinch a little. Some people don't feel a thing, but others say it feels like a little poke. Nobody's ever died in my chair," she said laughing.

I sort of wanted to leave, but I had come this far and I couldn't walk out the door a like little kid. Besides, I'd never get this chance again if I left. I got in the chair and said a prayer.

Michalina had me pick out a pair of earrings and told Faith the 14k gold ones were the best. She made a dot on each ear with a marker and asked me if the marks seemed straight. I nodded and she loaded the piercing gun. I took a deep breath and closed my eyes.

"Ready?" she asked.

I bit my lip and nodded. She placed the gun against my earlobe. *Punch!* It felt like she had stapled my ear. I put my hand up to see if I was bleeding.

"Are you okay?" Michalina asked. She and my aunt were staring at me. I wondered if I could go the rest of my life with one ear pierced or would it look weird? I decided to get it over with. Michalina pierced my left ear and it hurt worse than the right. I thought I was going to fall out of the chair from the pain.

"See? You hardly felt a thing," Michalina said.

Yeah, I loved feeling like the earth was swaying underneath me. My ears were throbbing, and I was so lightheaded Aunt Faith had to help me out of the chair. Michalina asked if we wanted to look at earrings, but I thought I might pass out and I wanted to go home. I leaned against the counter as my aunt paid. Michalina came over and gave me a hug. She reminded me to clean and turn my posts and gave me a bottle of cleaning solution.

"Are you okay?" Faith asked when we got in the car.

"It hurt worse than I thought. Still, I'm glad I didn't have Simone do it," I said.

"Ew." She shuddered. "Promise me you won't put any more holes in your ears. I don't want to see you in a month with three holes in each ear."

I promised I wouldn't get any more piercings. I wanted to say there was no way I'd ever go through that again, but I didn't want her to get upset. I had to act like it was no big deal so she wouldn't feel guilty for taking me behind my parents' backs. I flipped the visor mirror down so I could see the earrings.

"Do you regret it?" she asked.

"No, it looks nice, don't you think?"

She nodded and told me to drop hints to Grandma about wanting diamond earrings for my upcoming sixteenth birthday. I couldn't wait to show Simone. I wished I could have gotten cooler earrings. I didn't realize I was going to have to wait so long to change them, but as soon as I could, I was going to go downtown and buy a pair of dangly palm tree earrings like Simone's. Grandma was waiting by the door when we pulled up. She pulled my hair back with her hands.

"Maggie, do these studs look even to you?" she asked, squinting. My aunt rolled her eyes and said they were straight.

"Are you sure?" Grandma asked, tilting my head up. "They look off to me."

"Yes, Ma. Perfectly even. They look nice, Hadley," Aunt Maggie said. She held Lily up to see and Lily put her hands up to touch them. I backed away since my ears were already sensitive and I didn't need somebody swatting at me.

I called Simone to tell her about my ears, but she was in a weird mood.

"Do you want to come over?" I asked.

"I'm like, super busy. Maybe another time."

I went over to Charlotte's house instead.

"Why are you smiling so weird?" Charlotte asked.

I had put my hair in a ponytail so she could see my earrings better. "Notice anything?" I asked.

"Yeah, you're acting like a freak," she said.

"I got my ears pierced. Aunt Faith took me this morning," I said.

She peered closer and asked if it hurt. I didn't want to act like a kid so I said it didn't.

"It looks okay, I guess. I mean, if you like them that's all that matters, and at least you didn't let Simone do it," she said.

Her grandpa had made some lemonade and his hands shook as he poured it for us. He asked if I wanted to stay for lunch and said he'd make us mini pizzas. I called my Grandma's house to check and asked if I could have lunch over here. I was in luck because Aunt Maggie answered and said I would miss out on a fresh batch of her tuna salad.

"Oh, your friend Simone called," Maggie said. "She wanted to get together today."

I bit my lip. Simone wanted to see me. I could pretend I had to go home and then call her, but I did like spending time with Charlotte and her grandpa.

"So? Can you stay?" Mr. Lidstrom asked when I hung up the phone.

"Yup, sure can," I said. "Thanks for having me."

I decided to stay longer after lunch, and Charlotte and I worked on a collage she wanted for her wall of pictures from magazines.

I didn't call Simone until after dinner, and then, when she came over, she said Pilar and Morgan were acting weird around her.

"What do you mean?" I asked.

"Well, I went out to dinner and a movie with my mom the other night. Connor wanted me to come over and watch movies with Lucas, Nick, Morgan, and Pilar, but it was my mom's birthday, so I went with her instead," she said. "I mean, it would be wrong to leave her alone on her birthday."

"So what happened?" I asked.

Simone picked up Jack the Bear. "I'm not sure. All I know is Morgan told me we were going to have to find somebody new for me to like because Pilar was going out with Connor now."

"Wait—after *one* night?"

"Yup," she stared up at me with her round blue eyes. "I can't believe they would go behind my back like that. But you know, the other day we all went to the beach and she kept talking to him and touching his arm." She rolled her eyes. "She's so obvious. I think she's jealous because Lauren's coming to visit me."

I nodded.

"I swear, everything had been fine until the party. Connor kept trying to kiss me and I didn't mind at first, but then it seemed like it was all he wanted to do. I felt weird because he wanted to be alone and I wanted to go back to the party. He even called me a 'little girl.' What a jerk," she said, picking fuzz from the bear. "And I think Morgan only got him and Pilar together because Morgan and I had the same shorts on at the party, and Connor said I was hotter in them."

"Did he say it in front of her?" I asked.

"Not *right* in front of her, but I'm pretty sure she heard. And she didn't seem too thrilled when Nick started asking me questions about you. Then, when the guys went to watch a baseball game, they went past this channel that was showing a movie I was in years ago. I only had a tiny part in it, but Connor seemed impressed and I think it made Pilar and Morgan mad. I didn't even want to watch the stupid movie." She sighed and put Jack the Bear down. "I used to have a bear like this. Except mine was a girl bear with a princess hat."

"What happened to her?"

"I guess she ended up in the garage. I put a lot of

my kid stuff in boxes when we moved," she said.

"When did you guys move here?"

"A year ago, after I stopped working and then my parents got divorced. Sort of why I went out with my mom for her birthday." She pulled her knees up to her chest. "She's been upset because she found out my dad's marrying his girlfriend," she said.

I wasn't sure what to say, so I said it might be cool to have a new stepmom. However, that wasn't the right thing to say, because she gave me the coldest look.

"The woman will *not* be my stepmom," she said. "My dad never spends any time with me, but now he's talking about putting his house up for sale and getting a bigger place in case they have kids."

"Does he live nearby?" I asked.

"About a half-hour, but he never comes here. I *always* have to go there, and then he usually leaves to go out or something. The worst thing is my mom was pregnant two years ago." She sighed. "Then she lost the baby and my parents started fighting a lot."

Simone got super quiet and stared out the window until I suggested we walk down to the docks and get a Tropical Icy.

"I dunno. I don't want to run into my friends there. I'm not ready to deal with all that drama. It is cool if we stay in and watch TV or something?"

I nodded and we went downstairs and made root beer floats.

"This summer officially stinks," Simone said, licking root beer foam off her upper lip. "All my friends hate me, my dad's a jerk, and now I don't even have a boyfriend."

"Did Morgan sound mad when she called?" I asked.

"No, it's...I don't know how to explain her. She acts like she's your friend one minute, and then she says something totally mean to you. The day after the party we all had plans to go to the beach, but Morgan called and said they weren't going, so I stayed home." She licked the ice cream off the end of her straw. "But then I found out they went to the beach without me."

"That sucks. Do you want to do something tomorrow?" I asked. "We could go to the beach."

She said she didn't want to run into Morgan and Pilar, but she told me to call her tomorrow and we'd get together. "Oh, and Lauren will be in town soon, and we should all get together," she said. "Maybe we could invite Nick since he's obviously into you."

After she left, I planned what I would wear when I got to meet Lauren Gere. I pulled out my new journal with the wildflowers on the cover, and when I opened it, I realized it was a gratitude journal. Underneath the post, *Things to be grateful for,* I wrote:

1. Had fun with Charlotte and her grandpa 2. Hung out with Simone 3. Simone invited me to hang out when Lauren gets here 4. Finally being included in plans 5. New earrings 6. Getting to hang out with Aunt Faith 7. Spending time with Grandpa and watching soaps 8. Nick was asking about me 9. Best. Summer. Ever.

Chapter Ten

The next morning I woke up and saw I had two missed calls from Simone. I guess I had accidentally turned my ringer off when I went to bed. Charlotte called to see if I wanted to go downtown. I wanted to, but I told her I'd call her back after I asked my grandmother. Instead, I dialed Simone's number. I mean, she had called me first after all.

"Hello?"

"Hi, Mrs. Hendrickson, it's Hadley. Is Simone home?" I asked.

"Hi hon, no, she's not. Simone's out with her friends."

I guess they made up. Nice of Simone to let me know. I called Charlotte back.

"Hey, I am dying to go to the lighthouse museum. Wanna go?" Charlotte asked.

It sounded super boring, but she was so excited about it that I couldn't say no. We had to walk pretty far to get to it, but at least we got to go inside and look around. The guide said there were rumors it was haunted.

"What do the ghosts do?" I asked.

"Well, sometimes I hear somebody walking up the stairs, but no one's there and the lights turn on and off all the time," he said.

Not exactly the lighthouse of terror then. I was starting to feel a little claustrophobic, but Charlotte was in awe and taking pictures of everything. The air felt hot and stale, and I needed to get out of there. Finally, I told her I'd wait outside for her until she was ready. We walked down the boardwalk and decided to go to this spot that overlooked downtown Grand Haven. Some of the cottages were built right into the hills and were so high up they had these little elevator thingies to help the people get up the hill.

"I wish I lived in one of those," I said.

"Yeah, but most of the stores and restaurants close during the fall and winter because there aren't a lot of tourists and then it's not as much fun," she said. "Oh, see the huge brown house with the two tier deck in the front? That's Pilar's house."

The house was across the street from the beach and overlooked the lake. We started to walk back down to the beach when we saw Morgan and Pilar coming up the path. Pilar was wearing one of those strapless bathing suit cover-ups, which showed off her impossibly dark tan. I had seen the exact same cover-up in *Seventeen,* and I knew it cost a ton. I wondered which house Morgan lived in and figured it was probably the big blue one I had been drooling over. I started to say something to the girls as they got closer, but they walked past me without even looking in my direction.

Next Door To A Star

***

I called Simone the next day, but she was going over to Morgan's for lunch.

"I so want to talk to you though," she said, and my heart soared. "I'll be back around three, so call me then and we'll hang out."

After lunch, Charlotte called and invited me over to watch *Charmed Lives*. I wanted to tell her Nick had been asking about me again, but she had acted so weird the last time that I let it go.

After the show, Charlotte asked if I wanted to get some ice cream. I wanted to, but it was after three o'clock.

"Simone asked me to hang out later. You could come too," I said.

She wrinkled her nose. "Nah, I'm good. That's not really my scene. But you guys have plans, so no worries. We'll hang out another time."

I called Simone as I walked to the house.

Her mom answered. "Oh hi, hon," she said. "Simone's still out with her crew. I'll let her know you called. I think Nick's mom is flying home tonight, so it probably won't be too late."

Wait, she was with Nick too? The same Nick who supposedly wanted her to bring me along the next time they hung out? That sucked.

I decided to walk back to Charlotte's since I didn't have plans anymore, but when I got there, her grandpa said she left. I figured she probably went to get ice cream by herself and I could meet up with her at the parlor, but Grandma wouldn't let me go alone. Aunt Faith went with me, but Char wasn't there. I wondered where she was and if she was hanging out with someone else.

***

Charlotte didn't call me the next day either. I stayed in my room reading until it got too hot up there and went outside to read in the hammock. Uncle Stu asked if I wanted to go with him and the boys to play miniature golf, but I decided to go over to Charlotte's. Her grandpa let me in and I went into her room where there was another girl sitting on her bed looking through a scrapbook.

"Oh, hi," Charlotte said. "I didn't know you were coming over. This is Deidre."

Deidre stared up at me through her straight black bangs and nodded. Then she went back to the scrapbook. "Remember when we went tubing last year?" she asked, leaning closer to Charlotte.

They both cracked up and I tried to smile even though I had no clue what they were talking about. Charlotte explained Deidre's mom had convinced her to try tubing last year.

"I thought I was going to drown," Char said. "I fell out of the tube, but I kept hanging onto the rope thing and everybody was yelling at me to let go—"

"'Cause when you let go, you float up to the top," Deidre said.

"But I didn't know that and it was *so* funny," she said. "Well, except for the almost drowning part."

"Did you guys meet this summer too?" I asked.

They exchanged a look. "No, we've known each other for a long time," Charlotte said. "Deidre lives

Next Door To A Star

in Grand Haven. She's back from gymnastics camp."

"My cousins Pilar and Jeremy Ito live nearby," Deidre said. "Do you know them?"

Pilar was her cousin? Deidre sort of resembled Pilar, except she didn't have the super dark tan, the long hair, or the cheekbones. Deidre was what Pilar would look like without the platform sandals, tons of makeup, and cute clothes.

The two of them kept talking about school, and I felt so left out.

"We're going over to Deidre's house," Char said. I didn't know if I was invited or not from the way Deidre was looking at me.

"Oh, okay, well, I have to leave anyway because I'm going to play miniature golf with Clark and my uncle," I said, getting up.

I walked home and Grandpa said Uncle Stu had already left with the boys. I tried calling Simone's cell phone.

"Hi, it's Hadley. Is Lauren in town yet—?"

"Hadley, I gotta go," she said, interrupting me. "I'll call you later."

Simone never called back, and I ended up spending the night watching a baseball game with Grandpa.

"It's kind of nice to have a TV watching pal," Grandpa said smiling.

"Yeah, Dad watches the History Channel non-stop, and my mom could watch HGTV all day long. It's nice to have someone who understands my love of soaps and sports."

"And you understand baseball pretty well," he

said. "Your dad was never into it."

"Nope, Mom's the bigger sports fan, but she likes basketball more."

I heard my phone buzz with a text, but I didn't recognize the number.

Hey, it's Nick. Finally got your number from Simone. Hope it's cool that I'm messaging ya. I wanted to see what you were up to.

I almost dropped the phone I was so excited. I wrote back that I was watching a Tigers game with my grandpa and then winced because it looked lamer on the screen than it had sounded in my head.

Nick: No way, I'm watching with my dad right now. We got back from picking up my mom.

Nick and I texted back and forth about the game. It seemed easier to talk about baseball with him, but Simone hadn't told me exactly what he had asked her about me. Did he want a friend to talk to about sports or something, or was he interested in me?

Nick: Did you see the first baseman trip over his feet? I think we found our new role model in life.

I laughed and texted back.

Me: We might need to aim higher and go for someone who can run two feet without landing on his face.

Nick: You have loftier goals than me. See, I knew it—you're good for me. Making me aim higher.

I smiled and texted back a sticker of a girl prancing down a runway.

Me: I might be delusional if I think I could make it down a runway like her.

Nick: If anyone could do it, you can. So why haven't you come around with Simone? I've missed seeing you.

What to say? That I was never included in her plans? That I wasn't sure she saw me as what—an equal? I tried to think how to word it, while sounding mysterious and like someone he'd want to go out with.

Nick: Gotta go, Dad's yelling at me for not paying attention. ;) Talk to ya soon. Night.

"So…a boy?" Grandpa asked.
"How did you know?"
"You get that same look on your face that Faith does when a guy messages her." He laughed.
"I don't know if he's interested or not though. He might have wanted someone to talk to about the game. I mean, it seems like he's into me."
"If he was willing to take time away from the game to focus on you…my guess is that he's interested, and my advice is to not tell your

grandmother," he said with a wink.

Chapter Eleven

I called Charlotte the next morning to see if she wanted to come over, but she was going out on Deidre's dad's boat.

"I guess I can ask if you can come along," she said.

"It's okay. I might do something with my grandparents," I said. I didn't want to beg for an invitation.

"Oh, okay. Well, have fun," she said.

I spent all morning reading and hoping Simone would call me to do something and bring up Nick. I wondered if Lauren was in town yet.

Aunt Maggie came into my room. "I'm going to get my hair done downtown. You want to go with me? You could get a trim if you want and afterward we can get ice cream."

Grandma had been reading in the family room all morning, so it wasn't like I'd be able to watch *Charmed Lives* anyway. At least at the salon I'd be able to read magazines.

"Sure, thanks."

Aunt Maggie was getting her hair washed when

Simone came in with her mom. They both had appointments, but her mom went first so Simone sat down with me.

"I'm getting a trim and maybe some layers," Simone said. "I want to get highlights, but my mom won't let me because they fry my hair. I used to have them all the time though."

I wasn't exactly sure what all went into getting highlights other than using some kind of bleach and tinfoil, but I nodded. One of the magazines had said Valeria had buttery highlights near her face, so they had to be a good thing. Maggie came out with a towel on her head and asked if I wanted to get my hair cut. My hair was in a messy ponytail and needed a trim, but I'd only ever had one person cut my hair for me—my mom's hairstylist, Ramona. She had been doing my hair since I was little, and I was a bit nervous about the idea of someone else touching my hair.

"You should do it," said Simone. "You would look good with some layers around your face."

Valeria had layers around her face, so I agreed. Simone and I had our hair washed, and I felt dumb having her see me with wet hair. I always made sure never to get it wet at the beach when I was with her. However, Simone was even pretty with her wet hair plastered against her head.

"Okay, so we're doing layers?" the stylist asked me.

"Yeah, like this," I said, pulling up a picture of Valeria on my phone.

"Do you want a bit of bangs with it like in the picture?"

I looked over at Simone.

"Do it," she said. "If you hate it, they will grow out by the time school starts."

"Bangs like these are easy to blend in with the rest of the hair if you don't like them," the stylist said.

I nodded and she said she was going to use a razor on my hair. I didn't know what she meant and about had a stroke when she started using it around my face. I thought my hair would end up looking all choppy since the stylist kept cutting it away from the rest of my hair, but it fell right into place when she finished.

I looked at all the hair on the floor around my chair. She cut a ton off, but it was still sorta long, and now it had shorter pieces in front like Simone's. Simone's hairstylist told her to use a deep conditioner since she was bleaching her hair.

"Don't tell my mom, okay?" Simone said to me. "I use this stuff you spray in your hair to make it blonder. She won't let me highlight it anymore, and my hair's gotten darker in the last two years. I had to do something while the highlights grew out."

Her stylist told her she shouldn't use the bleaching stuff and said your hormones made your hair darker as you get older. Simone made a face when she said, "hormones." Adults always blamed everything on hormones. You could steal a car and back over a dog and they'd shake their heads and blame it on hormones.

"Where do you get that bleaching stuff?" I asked after the hairstylist left to get some styling pomade.

"They took it off the market, but I stockpiled

right before they did, so I have a ton left. It's super easy to use. I can do it for you," she said. "You have to use a hairdryer or sit in the sun to activate it. It looks pretty natural. Come over tonight and I'll show you."

I went over to her house after dinner and she sprayed something called "Sunglazing" in my hair. It smelled like rotten eggs and Windex, but I didn't complain. She used her hairdryer and my head felt tight and itchy from the heat. It didn't look much different when she was finished, but she said it would be more noticeable if I sat out in the sun.

"I use it a lot and my hair's naturally dishwater blonde. It's even darker than yours," she said.

I was surprised since my hair seemed a lot darker than Simone's. Her hair was super blonde now.

"Make sure you put more conditioner on your hair so it doesn't dry out," she said.

I didn't own any, but Lily had a bottle of Baby Tangles-Be-Gone which said, "extra conditioning" on the label so I figured I could use it.

"So what's going on with Connor and Pilar?" I asked.

"They're still going out, but I think Pilar told him not to talk to me anymore. He, like, won't make eye contact with me or anything. It's so weird."

"When's Lauren coming to town?" I asked.

"Hmm?" she said as she pulled down the side of her waistband to check out her tan. "My color is getting gross." She pulled up the bottom of her pink tank top. "I need to put more on."

"Put more of what on?"

"I use this self-tanning cream, but sometimes it wears off kinda splotchy," she said.

Now it made sense why she was so tan. I always wondered how she got so much color when she was always putting on sunscreen. Simone put her hair up in a bun with a headband to pull back the little hairs around her face. Then she rolled up the bottom of her shorts and covered herself in tanning cream, which made her look greasy. She padded over to her bed on her heels so her oily feet wouldn't stain the carpet.

"Now I have to sit without touching anything for two hours so it can dry. Can you turn on the radio?" she asked.

Simone's mom asked if I wanted to stay for dinner. They were having tuna casserole, which I hated, but I called and asked if I could stay anyway.

"Simone, don't get the tanning stuff on my furniture," her mother said.

"I won't, Ma."

"Well, you left a brown ring on my white couch last week," she said. "That stuff stinks."

Simone rolled her eyes and passed me a plate of casserole. I tried to eat as much of it as I could.

"Ma, did you use fat-free soup in this?" Simone asked.

Her mother shook her head. After dinner, we ate leftover birthday cake that had been in the freezer. I never realized how awesome frozen frosting tasted—it was like biting into chewy ice cream. Simone didn't seem to mind the cake wasn't fat-free. We went over to my grandparents' yard after dinner. Simone was still oily from her fake tan and didn't want to go inside and have anybody see her. The backyard smelled fresh and moist from the sprinklers watering the grass.

I turned to look at her. "So when is Lauren coming—"

"Oh man, I got some tanning stuff on my shorts. I gotta throw these in the wash," she said, tugging at the hem. "Be right back."

I took a couple pics of my new hair while I was waiting, and, in a moment of rare bravery, sent one to Nick, asking what he thought of my new look. The second I sent it, I felt stupid and wanted to take it back. Ugh, now I would look so shallow and desperate for his approval. How could I be so dumb?

Nick: Looks really pretty, but you did before too. Was watching the Tigers last night and thought of you.

My face got warm as I wrote back that was I thinking about him too when I watched the last game. Simone walked up then.

"What are you doing for the Fourth of July?" I asked when she sat down with her new shorts on. I was hoping she'd ask me to watch the fireworks with her, spend the night, and then we'd go get, well, not best friend necklaces, but something matching that showed we were friends like all the girls at my school in Goodacre had. It seemed everyone had matching something or other. Lexi and I had the same school bags, but that was it. I always wanted to have matching jewelry with someone—that feeling of belonging. I really hoped we would hang out on the Fourth. Maybe Lauren would be in town then and we could all hang out. Instead, Simone said she had plans.

"Pilar's parents are having everybody over to watch the fireworks from their place," she said. "They have people over each year because you get a better view from up on the hill."

I would have died for an invitation to Pilar's party, but I knew it wouldn't happen. Pilar had never even spoken to me. I wished Simone would offer to ask if I could come, but she didn't say anything. After all, Nick had mentioned it to her that she should bring me along, right? As I was getting up the nerve to ask her if she would, she said the mosquitoes were bothering her and she was going to go inside. I had the same sick feeling I always got when I missed my chance to do something. The feeling only got worse when I went inside.

"Hadley, did you see the new *Celebrity Snooper* blog today?" Aunt Faith asked. "Simone is in it with Lauren Gere."

"What? She didn't say anything about that. Were these super old pictures?"

"Here," she said. "I'll pull it up on my phone. It's Simone and Lauren walking along the boardwalk with some blonde girl and a boy."

"Does it say when that happened?" I asked. I couldn't believe Simone wouldn't have mentioned Lauren had already been here.

Faith found the site on her phone and stared at it. "I'm not sure, but I guess it was pretty recent. Here, look."

Simone was on the phone in the picture and the blonde girl with them was Morgan. But what was worse was that the boy was Nick and Lauren had her hand on his arm. Great, it was probably the same night I called Simone and she was too busy to talk. Maybe I was the one on the other end of the phone in the stupid picture. I had missed my chance to meet Lauren, and Simone never even told me when she was in town. I guess I wasn't cool enough for her to admit she was friends with me to somebody like Lauren. Who was I kidding? A TV star wanting to hang out with me? We weren't friends at all. I was somebody she ran to when she needed something. And Nick was probably humoring me until his new celebrity girlfriend called him back. I wanted to throw up all over the table.

"Didn't Simone mention it to you?" Aunt Faith asked.

"Maybe she did and I wasn't paying attention. I'm super tired, so I'm gonna go to bed. Night."

I went up to my room and cleared my clothes off my bed. The gratitude journal fell on the floor and I kicked at it with my foot. Here I thought I had finally made some new friends and it turned out one was using me and neither one of them cared enough to invite me to the Fourth of July party. I don't know why I thought I would fit in somewhere or that some great guy would like me. I guess I got lucky with Lexi, but now even she had forgotten about me. All her posts online were with new people, and she never tagged me or messaged me back. I guess I wasn't important enough to be anyone's priority.

Chapter Twelve

While Simone got ready for the party everyone but me was invited to, I went to the grocery store with my grandmother. Grandma went to buy stuff for our little family BBQ, and I went to check out the fake tanning creams. I stuck a bottle of self-tanning cream in the cart. I planned to tell Grandma it was sunscreen if she asked. It did have an SPF of 4 in it, after all. Charlotte's grandpa was talking to Grandma in the meat aisle when I came back to the cart with some ice cream.

"Judd Lidstrom's coming over tomorrow to watch the fireworks," she said. I was excited until she told me Charlotte was going to a party with her friend instead. Great, so the whole world would be at Pilar's house, and I'd be stuck home. Even Clark was going to the Ito's because he had become friends with Pilar's brother, Jeremy. Grandpa had bought sparklers for us. and Uncle Stu was going to grill hot dogs, but I wasn't exactly in the party mood...if you could call sparklers and hot dogs a party.

Charlotte called later and asked if I wanted to go

Next Door To A Star

with her to Deidre's aunt and uncle's party tomorrow. I went to put on my fake tan and imagined myself walking into the party looking all tan and gorgeous, and everyone would be wondering who I was and why they hadn't asked me to hang out with them before. Connor and Lucas would want my phone number, Nick would be begging me to go out with him, Simone would realize I was cool, and Morgan would want to be my friend.

Then reality set in. First, the fake tan squirted out of the bottle all gooey. I rubbed the cold cream all over my arms and legs and put a little on my face. Simone had said you had to wash your hands well or it would stain your palms. I wasn't sure how to put the tanning stuff on the back of my hands without getting it on my palms and drying, so I decided not to put any on my hands at all. I sat on some paper towels so I wouldn't get any brown stuff on my bed, but it seemed to dry fast.

I woke up the next morning and I was definitely darker. My face was kind of orange, but my arms and legs had streaks on them. It was like somebody had burned me with a curling iron. Plus, my hands looked like I had white gloves on compared to the rest of me. I couldn't go to the party all streaky. People would make fun of me. I thought about putting the tanning stuff on all the lighter places on my body, but then it might look like I had a disease. I ended up wearing a long sleeved shirt and jeans to the party. Charlotte had on a t-shirt and shorts when she came to pick me up.

"Aren't you hot wearing all that?" she asked.

"I want to be covered for the mosquitoes," I said. "Malaria is nothing to mess around with."

"I have some bug spray," she said. "But maybe I better bring a sweatshirt too. You got your hair chopped. It's cute."

I wasn't the only one wearing jeans at the party, but I felt like I was dressed for a winter carnival when I saw Morgan and Pilar. Pilar had a deep pink halter top on with tiny jean shorts, and she had put some shimmery stuff all over her arms and legs. Morgan was wearing a blue crocheted tank top, and she would have passed for at least seventeen. She had her curly blonde hair down for a change, and all the guys were sitting around her.

"She's so fake-looking," Charlotte said as we watched Morgan and Lucas dance.

Morgan seemed so confident as she moved her hips. I wouldn't be able to dance so free even if I was alone in my own bedroom. I was glad I had worn jeans because I would have seemed like a skinny kid next to Morgan's muscular legs. Simone was sitting next to Pilar and Connor, eating potato chips. Simone was wearing a black and white off the shoulder striped t-shirt and a jeans skirt. Nick was sitting off to the side drinking a glass of lemonade and watching the rest of the group dance. He didn't look my way at all.

Charlotte and I shared a lawn chair while Deidre sat on the porch rail. I ate hot dogs while I watched everyone else dancing and having fun. Deidre's uncle made cupcakes with red, white, and blue frosting, and Charlotte had eaten two cupcakes when I noticed her lips were purple from the frosting. I gave her my napkin to wipe her mouth, but she didn't seem to care.

"Hey, you going to ignore me all night?"

I looked up and Nick was standing there.

"Oh, hey."

"Can I sit?" he asked. I nodded. "So what's up?"

"Nothing."

"Hadley, did I weird you out when I said I was thinking about you the other night?" he asked.

"No, why?" I said staring at my hands.

"I dunno, you seem a little distant that's all. I didn't mean to come on too strong. I like you, that's all," he said. He looked a little sad, but how was I supposed to feel knowing he was only paying attention to me now that the TV star was back in L.A.?

"How's Lauren?"

He scrunched up his face. "Huh? Who?"

"Lauren Gere. I wouldn't think you could forget someone like her so easily."

"Oh, her. I dunno. Okay, I guess. She sent me a couple crazy texts."

"Define 'crazy texts,'" I said.

He laughed. "Um, well, in two of them she was wearing a bikini. I don't get texts like those every day."

Great. Very subtle, Lauren. "Are you guys going out now?"

"Nah," he said, looking out on the water. "I mean, she lives in L.A."

Lovely, so if it weren't for the distance factor, he'd be sending her love poems now.

"Besides, I like somebody else," he said.

I started to ask who when Pilar came over.

"We're getting ready for the fireworks display," she said, narrowing her eyes at Nick. I wondered if he wasn't supposed to be sitting with me. Nick turned to me when Simone rushed past us out of the house. She ran down the steps and Connor watched her, but he didn't go after her. Nick and I exchanged a look.

"It's kind of late for her to walk back by herself," I said. He nodded. I went to get Charlotte and we went after Simone.

"Leave me alone," Simone said when we caught up with her. Her mascara was smeared under her eyes and she moved away from us.

"Where are your shoes?" Charlotte asked.

Simone glanced down at her feet and said she left her sandals in Pilar's room. Charlotte offered to get them while Nick and I waited with Simone.

"What happened?" I asked her.

She looked over at Nick who said, "You know what? I'll go over here while ya'll...talk about...whatever."

As soon as he was out of earshot, Simone spilled. "They think I was flirting with Connor. It's so stupid," she said "Connor told me Morgan said I didn't like him anymore, so he asked Pilar out. I told him I never said anything to her about not liking him, and then Pilar accused me of trying to break them up."

"Why would Morgan say you didn't like him anymore?" I asked.

"I dunno. This summer has totally sucked," she said. We both stared up at the sky as the fireworks started.

"Oh, and they're mad I gave Nick your number, because, even though she won't admit it, Morgan likes to keep him around in case things don't work out with her and Connor. Nick's like, her backup. It's so dumb," she said.

Charlotte ran up holding Simone's sandals and Nick came back over. The four of us stood and watched the fireworks. Mosquitoes kept landing on Simone's arms, so Charlotte let her wear her sweatshirt. Simone sat on the curb and tucked her legs under the shirt, and I hoped Charlotte didn't notice Simone was wiping her nose on the sleeve.

"This must be the finale," Charlotte said as the sky lit up.

Nick touched my arm and moved me away from the girls. Charlotte was staring up at the sky and oblivious to everything around her.

"I'm really glad you came tonight, Hadley," he said.

"Me too. And thanks for coming with us to check on Simone. That was really sweet of you."

"Yeah, no problem, but I'm not sure if I should be insulted or not though," he said.

"Huh?" I turned to face him.

"I told you I liked somebody else, and you didn't even ask me who. Is it because you don't care or because you already know?"

I remembered Chandler had been in a similar situation on *Charmed Lives* and I quoted her word for word. "Well, don't keep it a mystery. Tell me."

He smiled and then leaned over and kissed me. I could smell the smoke from the fireworks mixed in with Nick's Polo cologne, and I thought I would pass out from happiness.

Then my inner dorkiness came out. "So it's me, right?" I asked.

He laughed. "Yeah, I thought you'd figure that out, but if you need clarification, that's cool."

I started laughing. "Sorry, I'm…yeah. Whatever."

"That's what I like about you. You're real. And for the record, I was never into Lauren. She was acting like she was super into me when she was here, but she's not my type at all. However, if you'd like to send me bathing suit pictures, I would not object at all," he said. "I'm kidding! Well, sort of."

He smiled and kissed me again, and when he pulled back, the fireworks show was ending.

"That was the best display ever," Charlotte said. I looked shocked until I realized she meant the fireworks and was oblivious to what had gone on literally behind her back. Even Simone didn't seem to notice that Nick and I had a major moment, but he was smiling at me, and it was like we shared this intimate secret.

Deidre came down and asked why we had run off without telling her. Charlotte told her we were walking Simone home and Deidre seemed disappointed.

"My uncle bought some fireworks and he's gonna shoot them off from the deck," Deidre said.

"I want to go home," Simone said. "You guys don't have to go back with me."

"Are you still spending the night?" Deidre asked Charlotte.

Next Door To A Star

Charlotte glanced over at Simone and me. I said I could walk Simone home and I noticed Deidre didn't seem to care whether or not I left.

"I'll walk you guys home," Nick said.

"But they'll get mad at you for leaving," Simone said.

He shrugged. "It's dark, and I want to make sure you guys get home okay."

My face got warm. He was so thoughtful. Unlike that jerk Connor who let Simone run out of the party upset and didn't even bother to check up on her.

Simone was texting Asia as we walked back and Nick reached over and held my hand. It felt like sparks were going off up my entire arm. We got to our street and I turned to thank Nick for walking us home.

"It was really sweet of you," I said.

"No problem," he said, glancing over to where Simone was standing. "Uh, well, I'll text you tomorrow then."

We both had stupid grins on our faces like we had some private joke. I wanted him to kiss me goodnight, but I also didn't want to share that sort of private moment in front of Simone.

"Will you tell me if they talk about me at the party?" Simone asked him.

"Oh, I'm going to head home," he said. "Less drama."

As soon as he walked away, Simone grabbed my arm. "Can I come over for a little bit? My mom will wonder why I'm home so early," she said. "And I don't want to have to get into it."

We walked through my backyard where Charlotte's grandpa was roasting marshmallows with my family.

"Hi, girls. Come make s'mores with us," Aunt Maggie said, handing Simone a stick with a marshmallow. Simone held it over the fire and Grandpa gave me a marshmallow, but I scorched it right away. Aunt Faith showed me how to turn it so the marshmallow was sort of bathed in the blue part of the flame.

"Simone, I saw you on the *Celebrity Snooper* site," Aunt Faith said. "That must have been a fun visit with your friend."

She shrugged. "Lauren flew home after the photographers showed up on the beach, and then Pilar got mad because they cut her out of all the shots."

I wanted to ask her more about it, but she'd already had a pretty rough night and I didn't want to make it worse.

We went into the kitchen and I started to pour her a diet soda when she asked if we had any regular soda. I found a can and she leaned across the counter and balanced herself on her stomach with her nose almost touching the countertop.

"I can't believe how those guys acted," I said. I was still hanging onto the hope this was it—the final fight, and now she'd realize I was her true friend and someone she could count on.

"They did it all the time at school last year," she said as she sat down and twisted her hair up. She grabbed a pencil lying near the phone and stuck it through the bun. I've tried that a million times and

I've never been able to get one to stay in my hair. Even with her hair all messed up and her eye makeup smeared, she still was like something out of a magazine. She sighed and spit an ice cube back into her glass.

"You know, Morgan used to get mad at my best friend, Asia, like, twice a week, so I'm used to it. They kissed my butt when Lauren was here, but now Lauren's gone so they don't need me anymore."

I shrugged. I wanted to say something about the fact she said she was going to introduce me to Lauren, but I wasn't brave enough. I guess I was lucky Charlotte hadn't gotten mad at me for all the times I dumped her to do something with Simone. Charlotte hadn't even abandoned me when Deidre came back to town. Maybe I'd even been lucky before when I only had Lexi for a friend. It seemed like having a lot of friends was a huge pain in the butt. I mean, I went out of my way to help Simone out, but there were tons of times when she told me we were going to hang out and then she left to do stuff with her popular friends...or her famous friends.

Simone and I went into the family room to watch TV and eat leftovers from my family's picnic. She finished off a container of potato salad and we polished off the rest of the raspberry gelatin. We made plans to go to the beach tomorrow when I walked her back to her place.

Chapter Thirteen

I went over to Simone's house at noon the next day. Her mom was rinsing off the dishes from lunch and Simone was on the back porch talking on the phone. She was telling her friend what happened at the party.

"Asia, they totally ganged up on me," she said. "And Connor did not say one word in my defense," she said. "Listen, I gotta go. Somebody's here."

Simone stood up and I followed her to her bedroom. She pulled her hair back into a ponytail and put a white shirt on over her aqua bikini top.

"Do you need sunscreen?" she asked. I nodded and rubbed some on. She even let me borrow a pair of pink flip-flops with big daisies on the front. We walked down to the beach and laid out our towels. She dug through her bag for some magazines.

"There's an article about Valeria in this one," she said, handing me a copy. "I'm going to get a skirt like hers when I get back to school."

"Her hair looks so different when it's long and curly," I said.

"Extensions," she said.

"Huh?"

"You know, when they sew fake hair in so your hair looks longer."

I didn't even know you could put fake hair in and make it look longer. I wondered how many of the people in the magazine had fake hair as I thumbed through it. I heard someone yelling, "No, Lucas! Stop it."

Simone was staring at Pilar, Connor, Lucas, and Morgan playing in the water. Lucas picked Morgan up and pretended he was going to throw her in the surf.

"I hope she drowns," Simone said. "Do you have any gum?"

I shook my head. I saw Charlotte and Deidre walking on the beach and wondered how their sleepover went last night. I felt a little queasy watching them together. Then Charlotte saw me and came over.

"I have your sweatshirt at home. I can give it to Hadley if you want," Simone said, squinting up at her.

Charlotte asked if we wanted to go with them to get sno-cones. I didn't bring any money with me, but Simone said she'd pay for mine. However, Connor was at the sno-cone stand with Pilar when we got there. Simone ignored them and walked up to the counter. She ordered two cherry sno-cones and then asked me if cherry was okay. I nodded as Pilar started talking to Deidre. Even Deidre was surprised her cousin was being so sweet to her.

"Did you guys have fun at the party?" Pilar asked us. It was the first time Pilar had ever spoken to me. We nodded and Simone kept her back to us.

"Hi, Simone," Connor said.

Simone stared at him. She said "hi" in a quiet voice and Pilar tugged on Connor's arm.

"See ya later, De," Pilar said over her shoulder as she and Connor walked away.

"Talk about awkward," Charlotte said.

Simone handed me my sno-cone and licked the drips off the side of hers. We stood on the docks and all you could hear were slurping sounds.

"We're going to go back to Deidre's house to watch a movie. Do you guys wanna come?" Charlotte asked.

"Um, my cousin and her friends are supposed to come over later for a barbeque," Deidre said.

She didn't come right out and say Simone wasn't invited, but Deidre made it clear Simone wasn't welcome. Charlotte gave me a pleading look, but Simone was already walking away so I shrugged and followed her.

"Call me tonight, Char," I said over my shoulder as I tried to catch up to Simone. I wondered if Nick was going to be at that party.

"You didn't have to come with me. You could have gone with them," Simone said.

I thought she was going to say she didn't want me tagging along, but she didn't say anything else as she smoothed more sunscreen on. She stretched out and put on her sunglasses. I asked if I could borrow some more sunscreen and she didn't answer. I nudged her with my toe and realized she had fallen asleep. I picked up a magazine and spent the afternoon reading. I went home with a headache from being out in the sun too long and my shoulders had started to peel. Simone and I hadn't talked much, but at least she wanted me around, and maybe she had planned to introduce me to Lauren but couldn't because she had to leave early. Maybe we'd end up being best friends yet.

Chapter Fourteen

By Saturday, Simone and her friends had made up and Nick still hadn't texted me. I went over to Simone's house to pick up Charlotte's sweatshirt since Simone never brought it over like she said she would. Pilar was painting her nails on Simone's bed and didn't even bother to look up, but Morgan stared at me. Simone gave me the sweatshirt and I realized she hadn't washed it because it still had mascara stains on it. I got out of there fast and took it over to Charlotte's house. We ended up going on a nature walk and I realized how much I missed spending time with her. Plus, it was nice to do something without Deidre around. Charlotte picked some white flowers and when we got to my grandparents' house, she asked if she could use my glitter pen to decorate the flowers.

"I can't believe school starts in three weeks," she said, lying across the foot of my bed.

My stomach rolled over. I had forgotten about school. Now I was going to face another year of torture.

"At least we still have some time to hang out

Next Door To A Star

before we have to go back," I said.

She shook her head. "My grandpa signed me up to go to some stupid music camp for a week. I begged to go to science camp, but I don't want to spend a week playing the violin indoors," she said.

"You're leaving? But we haven't even seen each other lately," I said.

"I know. You've been with Simone, but we'll have to hang out a lot this week," she said. "Hey, your hair looks lighter. Did you do something to it?"

"Simone put some stuff in it," I said. I went to the mirror. My hair did look a little brighter around my face. I was surprised Grandma hadn't said anything.

Char picked up her sweatshirt. "Ew, she didn't even wash it. It smells like cocoa butter and shampoo," she said.

I knew it was Paul Mitchell shampoo because I had peeked in Simone's bathroom cabinet.

"Nick and I kissed on the Fourth of July," I said.

She stared at me. "Seriously?"

"Yeah, I really like him, and I thought he liked me too, but he hadn't messaged me once since then."

She looked away. "Well, that crowd…I dunno. I wouldn't spend too much time thinking about him."

"But I—"

"I gotta get ready to go to Deidre's. I'll try to call you later, okay?" she said, getting up.

I ran into Simone as she was cutting across our lawn. She seemed kind of embarrassed, and I told her Charlotte was leaving tomorrow to go to music camp.

"Who?" Simone asked.

"The girl with the dark hair," I said. "She lent you her sweatshirt," I said.

"Oh yeah. Duh. Of course, she was in my math class last year. I gave it back, right?" she asked and I nodded.

"I'd hate to be stuck at some loser camp," she said. "Oh, I saw on *Celebrity Snooper* Jack Brogger is planning a vacation, and it sounds like he's coming here. The reporter said an unnamed source said Jack spent last summer at a lake resort in Michigan and he was going up there at the end of August. Dude, we've got to see him."

I asked if she wanted to come in, but she had to get home because she had met some guy at the beach and she thought he might call her when he got home. Aunt Faith asked if I wanted to split a brownie when I came in the house.

"Did you have fun with Charlotte last night?" she asked.

"We had a good time." My eyes started to water and I wiped them with the back of my hand.

"You're going to miss her a lot," she said.

"Yeah, my best friend moved to Texas a couple of months ago, and now I have to leave Charlotte," I wiped my nose on my sleeve.

"Charlotte's going to miss you. It's been hard for her since her mother passed away." She passed me a napkin. "Oh, Charisma might come for a visit soon."

I sat up. Charisma was coming here? I asked when, but Aunt Faith wasn't sure. "I don't know when she's getting back from her trip. I know she wants to come before she starts college. She probably won't have time though."

With my luck, Charisma would show up on the same day Jack Brogger came to town. They'd meet, and he'd look past the fact she had no personality and put her in his video, and they'd get engaged, and he'd give her a big sapphire ring like the one Chandler's character wore. Then they'd be on the cover of *InTouch Weekly* and there'd be pictures of them sitting at outdoor cafes, holding hands and drinking coffee, kissing on the beach all the time, acting as if they didn't know a photographer was there taking the picture. I never understood how none of the celebrities ever seemed to know there was a photographer around yet they looked perfect in the pictures.

"Hadley, do you want to split another brownie? I'm still hungry," Aunt Faith said. I shook my head. Charisma had a way of taking my appetite away. I went upstairs and curled up under the covers. I realized I hadn't finished Charlotte's copy of *The Lion, the Witch, and the Wardrobe*, so I read until I fell asleep.

Simone called the next morning to tell me Morgan was having a barbecue.

"It's this afternoon and her dad's going to grill. It should be fun. Do you want to go with me?" she asked. "Nick's going to be there and he told me to invite you."

I started to answer when I got a call on the other line.

"Hey," Charlotte said. "My grandpa's making a

special lunch for my last day. Can you come over?"

It was my last chance to see Charlotte, but Simone had never invited me along to a party, and it had been my dream to hang out with Morgan and her friends. Plus, Nick had remembered I still existed.

"Are you still there?" Charlotte asked.

"Yeah, sorry I'm out of it," I said. No, I couldn't miss out on seeing Charlotte before she left. I asked Charlotte what time I should come over and she told me to come right away. I got on the other line and told Simone I couldn't go.

"C'mon. Puh-lease?" she said. "Nick will be there and you can borrow one of my outfits. I don't want to go by myself. What if they get all weird on me again? Please?"

"It's the last time I'll see Charlotte," I said. "But maybe we can do something tomorr—"

"Whatever," she said and hung up.

I walked over to Charlotte's house and Mr. Lidstrom had put flowers from his garden in little glass jars at each of our plates. Deidre wasn't there yet so we went into Charlotte's room.

"I made something for you," she said.

She handed me a notebook that she had filled with stuff we'd done during the summer. There were pressed flowers from the walks we took, a picture of Valeria because we had spent so much time watching *Charmed Lives*, and pictures of book covers on one page. There was even a picture of Jack with question marks around his head saying, "Where are you?" And she had glued an envelope on the last page, and inside it was the necklace we had started to make out of gum wrappers.

"I can't believe I didn't finish it after all the gum I chewed," she said. It was too small to be a necklace, so I wore it as a bracelet.

"This is much better," I said. "And for once having skinny arms pays off."

Deidre came over and Mr. Lidstrom dished out lasagna, which was Charlotte's favorite. He had put vegetables from his garden in the salad, and we had little cheesecakes for dessert. Charlotte's bus came to pick her up at four o'clock. She gave us all hugs and waved to us from the window. We watched until the bus was out of sight.

"Would you girls like to stay for a while and have a glass of soda pop?" Mr. Lidstrom asked, looking hopeful.

Deidre said she had to leave, but I stayed and he poured me a glass of orange soda and put some cookies on a plate for us. We watched TV for a while, and I helped him in his garden until my grandpa came over.

"I see you've put my granddaughter to work," Grandpa said.

"She's a big help and good company," Mr. Lidstrom said.

"We're going to miss Charlotte around here," Grandpa said. Mr. Lidstrom made me promise to come back and visit him.

I was hoping Deidre might start calling me since Charlotte was gone. I even thought about calling her until I went to the beach with Aunt Faith and saw her hanging out with Pilar. I said "hi" to Deidre and she answered me, but she didn't go out of her way to be friendly. I noticed Simone wasn't with them, so I called her figuring she might want me around if her other friends were mad at her.

"Hey, what's up?" I asked.

"I'm so bored I could die," Simone said. "Do you want to go to the movies?"

We went to see *Death Comes for the Dress Up Dolly*, but she spent most of the movie sitting low in her seat and texting. I kept looking behind us to see if anyone was going to get up and yell at her for texting during the movie, but there weren't a lot of people in the theater.

The lights came on and I asked what she thought of the movie.

"Oh, dunno." She shrugged. "That doll was super creepy though. But guess what? Morgan and I just made up. It was all this huge misunderstanding. I feel so dumb. She is the best. So glad that's sorted."

Great, so I was back to hanging around the house and reading until they dumped her again.

That night I sent Nick a text before I went to bed.

Me: Hey, long time, no talk. The Tigers are doing pretty well. How are you doing? Miss ya.

But when I got up the next day, there was no message.

Chapter Fifteen

On Tuesday, I went to visit Mr. Lidstrom. His door was open and I saw him cleaning up the kitchen through the screen door. He had the radio on as he swept the floor and he invited me in and gave me a glass of root beer. He had to take some stuff up to the attic and I went up with him. Their attic was full of trunks and boxes and he said a lot of them were filled with his wife's things. He found a box of old photo albums and showed me pictures of Charlotte's mother and her grandmother. Charlotte resembled her grandma, but with darker hair. Mr. Lidstrom also had a stack of old supermarket tabloids.

"They're my guilty pleasure," he said. We spent the afternoon looking through the tabloids, and he let me keep all the ones with pictures of Jack Brogger and Josh Haven.

Clark was bugging his dad to take him to the movies when I got home. Uncle Stu gave in and asked if I wanted to come along. He said I could bring a friend since Clark was bringing three, but Simone wasn't home, so I went alone. We were standing in line when I saw Deidre by the snack counter with Pilar and her brother. Deidre told me both their families were going to Disneyland for a week. I wondered if it meant Connor would start going out with Simone when Pilar left. I hoped Simone would invite me to do stuff with her since Pilar was leaving and because she and Morgan were always fighting.

Of course, it didn't happen because Simone's best friend, Asia Milanowski, came back home from her vacation. I still kept thinking Simone would call me, but she didn't. Aunt Faith saw I was dying of boredom one afternoon, so she took Lily and me to get ice cream. Lily was fussing in her stroller so we took her out. Lily started running all over the place the second her feet hit the ground. Aunt Faith handed me her ice cream cone and took off after her as Morgan, Asia, and Simone walked into the ice cream shop. I was holding two cones and Morgan smirked at me.

"Eat enough?" she said. Simone said "hi" to me as Aunt Faith came back with Lily who was covered in chocolate ice cream.

"I've got to get her cleaned up," she said as Lily flailed her chocolaty arms and got a smudge on my beach t-shirt.

Morgan found this hysterical and Simone rolled her eyes. I didn't know if Simone was making fun of me or not, so I went outside with the ice cream to wait for my aunt. Simone came outside and handed me some napkins. She didn't say anything and went back inside. Aunt Faith came out ten minutes later with a wet paper towel for my shirt. The chocolate stain smeared and she told me she'd put it in the wash when we got home. I didn't even care. I had bought the t-shirt to look cool in front of Morgan and her friends, but it didn't matter because nothing I did was going to help me fit in with them.

I went up to my room to lie down and knocked my magazine off the bed. I picked it up and flipped to the article with Valeria, and I realized she was wearing hair extensions in almost all of the pictures. Then I noticed her eyes were brown in some pictures and blue in others. I wondered if Simone knew Valeria wore colored contacts. I'd been trying so hard to look like Valeria, and now I found out even Valeria didn't look like Valeria.

Simone called me the next day and asked me to come over. I figured she needed me to cover for her so she could go to a party, or maybe Morgan and Asia were mad at her, but they were both there when I walked into her room.

"Hi, Hadley," Simone said. "Do you want something to drink?" I noticed Simone was back to drinking diet Coke again. Morgan was looking through a magazine and Simone stuck her finger in the magazine and flipped the page back to show me a picture of Valeria.

"I love her hair in this picture," she said, pointing to a photo of Valeria with her hair cut like Simone's.

"Oh my God, are you trying to copy her?" Morgan said, cracking up. "How funny! You are so crazy."

Simone laughed it off and started picking her nail polish off. I asked if I could try her eyeliner on and she nodded.

"You use drugstore makeup?" Morgan asked, wrinkling her nose.

"All the makeup artists I worked with in L.A. used this kind," Simone said as she handed me her eye pencil.

"Oh, you're such an expert. I forgot what a big star you are," Morgan said, rolling her eyes.

"Valeria Joseph uses Be Lashful stuff too," I said.

"Well, she gets paid to say she uses it," Simone said. "I'm not sure she actually does."

I guess it would explain why Valeria's skin looked dewy and perfect in the ads and mine was more on the greasy side. My hand wasn't steady, and I smeared the liner under my right eye. Morgan snorted when she saw it, and I went to the bathroom to wash it off.

"We're going over to my house," Morgan said when I came back into the room. I was excited I was going to see Morgan's house.

"Okay, great," I said.

"Yeah, so...see ya later," Morgan said, looking me up and down. My stomach fell as I realized I hadn't been invited, and I made a fool of myself by letting her know I thought I had been.

"Um, I think I'm gonna stay here," Simone said. Morgan stared at her. "I'm kind of tired."

"Fine," Morgan said. "C'mon, Asia." Asia got up and followed her. After they left, Simone made some popcorn. She put a bag in the microwave, but she wasn't paying attention and it burned.

"Ma, how long do you put this stuff on for?" Her

mother came into the kitchen and opened the microwave door. Steam poured out of the microwave and her mother sighed.

"Let me do it, okay?" her mother said. Simone backed away and her mom heated up a bag of popcorn for us. We took the popcorn back to her room and she told me she had gotten sunburned yesterday.

"I burn fast, so I use the fake tanning stuff," she said as she smeared some aloe moisturizer on her cheeks. "Morgan was driving me nuts this morning. She told me my hair was starting to look cheap and maybe I should have it done professionally, and Asia sat there and said nothing."

"Your hair looks nice. Morgan's probably jealous," I said.

"I dunno. My mom thinks Morgan looks like a photo negative because her hair's so light and she's so tan. You know, she even goes to a tanning booth in the winter," she said.

"Why would anybody want to be tan in the winter?" I asked. "All you see in the winter are your face and hands."

"Morgan wears shorts until there's snow on the ground," Simone said. "Anyway, she wants me to go out on Lucas's family's boat with her, Nick, and Connor this weekend."

I asked if her mom would let her go and she shrugged. As much as I would be thrilled to have Morgan ask me to go anywhere with her, I'd be scared to death to go out on a boat with three guys. Simone was only a few months older than me, yet she seemed so much older and more mature. Maybe it was because she had been on TV. I said she could say she was coming over to my grandparents' house again if she wanted.

"Thanks. My mom would freak if she knew I was going to be on a boat with a bunch of guys, and Lucas's brother is nineteen." She played with the fringe on her shorts. "I don't even know if I want to go."

"Why not?" I asked, passing her the popcorn bowl.

"Well, Connor didn't exactly stick up for me when Morgan and Pilar got mad at me, and he's always trying to get me alone," she said. "Pilar hasn't even been gone a week and he's already called and told me he liked me all along, but Morgan wanted him to go out with Pilar. I mean, why didn't he tell her he liked me?"

"Yeah."

"And Asia's been kissing up to Morgan so bad. She's like her shadow now." Simone leaned back against her pillow.

"Has Nick mentioned me at all?" I asked.

"No, why?"

I didn't want to tell her about the kiss and then find out he now had a girlfriend or something.

"He stopped texting me."

"Boys are weird. Guess what? I found out my dad and his girlfriend are having fireworks at their stupid wedding."

"When did you find out?" I asked.

She said her dad had called last night. He wanted her to be a bridesmaid at his wedding, but he was getting married in September and she said she didn't think she could go.

"I'd have to miss two days of school because they decided to get married on Mackinac Island," she said.

"It's too bad your mom won't let you miss school," I said.

"Well, she said I could go if I wanted to, but I don't think I want to." She pulled another thread off her shorts and wound it around her finger. "They're already talking about having kids. They're not even married yet and his girlfriend was saying she'd love to have a baby named Dakota. Seriously?"

"It's a pretty name," I said.

"It's my grandmother's maiden name and my middle name," she said. "Why did she even bring that up, and of all the names in the universe? She's already got my dad, so why does she have to steal my name too?"

I didn't know what to say, so I offered to go refill the popcorn bowl. She seemed a little calmer when I came back.

"You know the bear you have?" she asked. "I found mine last night. She was in the garage. I went out there after I talked to my dad...I didn't want my mom to know I was upset."

She brought her bear out and it reminded me of Jack, but with a pink tutu on. I asked what her name was and she made a face.

"I named her Glitter. She was my mom's, but I liked her better than any of my bears. I showed her to Asia, and she said Glitter seemed kinda dirty. Maybe I should throw her in the wash," she said, staring at the bear's face. "But she doesn't look dirty to me."

Grandma called me to come home for dinner, but she said I could invite Simone over to eat. After dinner, we went up to my room. Simone loved my Jack Brogger sticker, and she said I could borrow the CDs of his I didn't already have, which was good because my mom wouldn't let me buy his *Livin' in Sin* album for some reason. I thought about buying it here since she wasn't around, but my mother had this way of being able to tell when I've done something wrong, and I knew she'd find out. Sometimes it was like my mother was psychic or something.

"I think Jack's hot, but I'm in love with Josh Haven. He's my favorite actor," she said. "I loved the movie he did with Angelia Byatt."

I hadn't seen it because I looked too young to get into R-rated movies without my parents—it was so embarrassing, but I nodded anyway.

"You know what we should do?" she said. "We should have a Josh movie marathon tonight. We could rent a bunch of Josh's movies, and you could spend the night."

It was okay with her mom, and Grandma said I could spend the night but not to "make a pest of myself." Simone and I got her mother's rental card and we went downtown. We got three Josh movies and then stopped for slushies at the ice cream parlor. I wanted a cherry cola slushie so I put both cola and cherry flavors in my cup. Simone thought it was a good idea so she put some of each in her cup too. We walked past the pizza place and I saw Morgan sitting at a table with Asia. I hoped Simone

Next Door To A Star

wouldn't notice them. She was having fun with me and I didn't want her missing her old friends, but she saw them and rolled her eyes.

"It's gonna be another fun school year," she said. "I'm so sick of it. Every year is the same. Somebody gets mad at me and then they're all mad at me. Then Morgan gets mad at somebody else and we all have to get mad at them, even if they didn't do anything to us," she said.

I thought she'd be depressed because her friends had gone out without her, but she seemed okay. One of the movies was stupid, so we fast forwarded through it and only watched the parts Josh was in. Josh wasn't a great actor, but he had this sort of dumb but sweet quality about him which made me like him.

"Wouldn't Josh and Valeria be a cute couple?" she asked. "Much better than the girl he pretends to be dating."

"Wait, *pretends* to date?"

"Yeah, you know, like those photos in the magazines where he's got his arm around that girl."

"So those aren't real?"

"When I was on the set everyone talked about how the studios had a deal with this one magazine to promote their stars. So the photographers from that magazine always knew who was going to be where, and everyone could look amazing in the shots."

It was weird to know it was all fake. I felt dumb falling for it, so to show her I wasn't super naïve, I told her I thought Valeria wore colored contact lenses and she sat up on the couch.

"For real? I never noticed. I think you're right though," she said. "You know what? Last week Morgan said everybody tells her she looks like Madison on *Charmed Lives*, but Lucas's brother said Madison was way taller. She got so mad and I felt bad for her. Not like she's ever stood up for me."

We slept in until noon. Simone's mom said there wasn't anything decent in the house for lunch and gave us some money to go downtown. Simone let me borrow a pink t-shirt and a pair of jean shorts when we walked to the hot dog stand and stopped for slushies. Nick was at the hot dog stand with another girl. I immediately shrank behind Simone when I saw him. She raised her eyebrows at me.

"Hey, Nick, what's up?" she asked.

He shrugged. "Nothing."

The girl had dark hair and wore cat eyeliner that made her look sophisticated—like a dark-haired version of Madison on *Charmed Lives*. The girl had an immaculate white sundress on, and I felt like such a slobby kid next to her.

"We haven't talked to you in a while," Simone said, squinting as she put her hand up to block the sun.

"Yeah," he said and then turned to the girl he was with and put his arm around her. "See ya around."

I felt like puking on the sidewalk. He had a new girlfriend and I was nothing to him now.

"What was that?" Simone asked as they walked away. "He's normally, like, super sweet. And who's that chick?"

"Maybe I did something wrong," I said. My eyes filled with tears as I told her about the kiss.

"But he was fine after that?" she asked.

I nodded. "And then all of a sudden he stopped texting me, and I wrote him, but got no response, so I stopped."

"Who knows? Maybe he got scared off. Don't worry about it. After all, we still have one Josh movie left," she said, putting her arm around my shoulder. "We don't need local boys when we have our Joshie."

Maybe she didn't, but I really liked Nick. He was the first guy I felt comfortable with, and he seemed like he liked me too. I couldn't figure out what I did wrong.

"Do you think that text I sent him weirded him out or something?" I asked.

She took my phone and scrolled through our messages. "I dunno, nothing jumps out at me. I don't understand boys though, so you are asking the wrong person."

***

Later, when Grandma called me to come home for dinner, I asked if Simone could eat with us.

"Fine, but we're having leftovers," Grandma said.

Grandma wasn't kidding when she said "leftovers." She and Grandpa had cleaned out the fridge. Simone and I pigged out and then we went up to my room and Simone went to my books.

"I used to read all the time, but when I moved

here I stopped. Oh my gosh, you have *The Fault in Our Stars*," she said. "I loved that. I read it a couple years ago and I cried so hard when I got to the end."

"I haven't finished it yet," I said.

"Don't skip ahead. You have to read the whole thing. Can I borrow it when you're done? I want to read it again," she said.

Aunt Faith came upstairs and said Mrs. Hendrickson was on the phone. Simone went to talk to her and she came back with a funny look on her face.

"My mom's going on a date tonight," she said. "She hasn't gone out with anybody since the divorce."

Aunt Faith asked if she wanted to stay over tonight and she nodded and went to call her mom back.

"Mom said I could stay, and I have my key so I can get my stuff," she said, sitting on the edge of my bed.

Grandma said we could sleep in the living room, but we were both pretty sore after sleeping on the floor the night before and we decided to sleep in my bed. I hadn't shared a bed with anyone since I was little and I hoped I wouldn't kick her in my sleep. She told me not to worry and said she was a blanket hog. She fell asleep pretty fast, but I stared up at the ceiling, wondering who Nick's new girlfriend was and what she had that I didn't.

Chapter Sixteen

My parents decided to come to Grand Haven a week early. They hadn't told me they were coming, but my grandparents didn't seem surprised. Oh well, it would be a good distraction to get me over my Nick heartache. Mom noticed my earrings right away, but she didn't seem too worried about it. Grandma told my parents she had nothing to do with it, and Aunt Faith rolled her eyes at me. They brought me a peach sweatshirt with "Toronto" on it and a charm bracelet. Dad asked if I had been having a good time, and I told them about hanging out with Charlotte and Simone.

"Well, I'm glad you like it here, because your mother and I have been talking, and we've been thinking about moving here," he said. "Mr. Stevens has been looking for someone to manage the office here and we thought it might be a nice change," he said. "It was part of the reason Grandpa wanted you to come for a visit."

I was confused, because I had been dreading going back to my old school, but I wasn't sure if I was ready to start over in a new school. Of course,

I'd have Charlotte here, and I didn't have any friends I was leaving back home. Plus, Simone and I had become closer, but I wasn't sure if she'd want to hang out with me once school started. She said she and her friends got into fights all the time, but then they always made up. Maybe I wouldn't be cool enough for Simone to hang out with once we got to school. Plus, now there was all the weirdness between me and Nick.

"We found a place nearby for rent," Dad said. "So we thought we'd come back a little early to get the paperwork taken care of. You and Mom can go home and pack up the rest of the stuff while I get things settled here with the house and my new job."

I called Simone to tell her my news, but she was crying when she answered. She had found out Morgan had taken Asia to go to Cedar Pointe with her.

"Morgan's family goes each year before Labor Day, and she *always* asks me to go," she said. "I talked to her yesterday and everything was fine, but I called Asia's house today and her mom told me where they were."

We talked for a few minutes and I told her I was moving. She said she'd help me fix up my room, and she seemed sorta excited about it when I left with my mom to go back to Goodacre to pack up the house.

***

Once we were back in Goodacre, I started to feel a little sad about leaving my old room. I didn't know if our new house was going to be big enough for all of our stuff, but Mom said we were going to store stuff at my grandparents' house. The movers were loading our furniture into their truck and Mom asked if there was anyone I wanted to see before we left. The only person I had hung around with after Lexi moved was Jennifer…and the school nurse. I shook my head.

"Will you run down the street to Foodies and get some more boxes?" Mom asked. I stopped to put on some lip gloss in case I ran into anyone while I was there.

"Pick up some soda pop while you're there," she said, giving me some money. "I can't get used to you with this new haircut and those bangs. It's cute though. You look a lot older. Guess you won't need me to buy those R-rated movie tickets for you now."

"Very funny," I said as she laughed.

I walked into the store, saw Brittany and Isabella over by the magazines, and I walked right back out. My heart was racing, and it felt like it was going to jump out of my chest. I had been feeling pretty confident lately, well, for me anyway, and I was not going to let Brittany bring me down. I was about to turn around and go home when I decided I had nothing to lose. Even if Brittany spit in my face, it wouldn't matter, because I was moving and I would never have to see her stupid face ever again. I went back into the store and walked right past them. They didn't even notice me. I got the boxes and soda and was on my way to the checkout counter when I like, flipped out or something. I don't know what happened to me, but I walked over to where they were looking at magazines and said, "Hi, Isabella."

"Hey," she said, squinting at me. "Oh, hi, Hadley. I almost didn't recognize you. You cut your hair. It looks good."

Brittany didn't say anything, so I told them I was moving to Grand Haven because my dad got a job in Spring Lake.

"Oh, cool," Isabella said. "It'll be weird having to make new friends though."

Brittany rolled her eyes.

"Actually, I've met a ton of people there. You know the show *Duncan's Corner*?" I asked. Isabella nodded, but Brittany sighed. "Well, I'm friends with the girl who played Abby. She lives next door to my grandparents."

Brittany didn't say anything, but Isabella's eyes almost popped out of her head. "Seriously? Let me give you my e-mail address so we can keep in touch. Brit, do you have a pen?"

Brittany glanced in her purse and said she didn't have one in a bored voice.

"It's okay," I said. "I barely have time to text or e-mail anyway."

"Hold on," Isabella said, running up to the service counter to borrow a pen. She wrote her address on a scrap of paper and gave it to me.

"So what's Abby like?" she asked.

"Abby? Oh, you mean *Simone*," I said. "She's cool, and she spent the night. Well, actually, I spent the night at her house, and then she came over to my house. Anyway, I gotta go. We're leaving today. Have fun in school, guys."

As I walked away I thought about how we had gone to school together for years and she had never bothered to get my e-mail or phone number before. I considered throwing Isabella's e-mail address away. After all, she didn't want to be my friend when she had the chance. She only liked me now because of who I knew, not who I was, and that hurt. But two things stopped me— although Isabella didn't stick up for me, she was never mean to me. She didn't deserve me acting that way toward her. And second, I overheard Brittany say, "She's such a liar. She doesn't know her." So I decided I'd e-mail Isabella some pictures of me with Simone.

Chapter Seventeen

Mom and I went back to Grand Haven and started moving our furniture into the new house. It was a tall brown house, which was built into the hill. You had to walk up a long staircase to get to the front door, and the garage was right on the street. It was a street over from Grandma and Grandpa's house.

"These stairs are going to be treacherous in the winter." Grandma shuddered. "Remember, we get more snow because of the lake effect."

The house wasn't as nice as our old house in Goodacre, but it was cozier. There was a brick fireplace in the family room, a screened-in porch which overlooked the trees, and a walkout basement. Even my grandparents' house didn't have one of those. There was one bedroom with ugly rooster wallpaper, but it had a great view. You could almost see the lake through the trees if you squinted hard enough. Mom said it could be my room, but even Dad said we would have to paint it because the rooster paper was so ugly.

Mr. Lidstrom waited to let me tell Charlotte we

had moved. She was surprised to see me when her bus dropped her off. Originally, I was supposed to have gone back to Goodacre by now.

"My parents decided we're going to move here," I said.

"No way! You're kidding," she said. "Are you going to live with your grandparents?"

"Well, I'm staying there now because our place isn't ready yet, but we got a house on Anthony Street."

"How cool. Will you be going to Watson too?" she asked.

Mom had already talked to someone at Watson High School, and all I knew was I was in Mrs. Feldman's homeroom. She asked her grandpa if her room assignment card had come yet. We checked it, but she was in Mr. Chang's room.

"I hope we have lunch together," I said.

"There's only one lunch period."

"Oh wow, I didn't realize it was such a small school. Well, then I hope I don't have any classes with Pilar or Morgan," I said.

"I was Pilar's lab partner last year."

I thought it was strange they had been lab partners since Pilar had barely spoken to Char all summer. Charlotte was exhausted, so I went back to Grandpa's house and Simone came over. She was in Mrs. Feldman's room too, but Pilar, Morgan, and Asia were all in Mr. Chang's room.

"Life is so unfair," she said. "My mom already said it might be a good opportunity to meet new people. How lame," she said. "But she said she'd take me to the mall in Spring Lake tomorrow to get some new school clothes. Do you wanna come?"

Mom gave me some money and so did Grandma, who told me not to buy anything, "too short, too revealing, or cheap-looking, and don't spend all your money."

***

Simone's mom picked me up at ten o'clock. Mrs. Hendrickson stopped to get gas and gave us money to get a soda. Simone was back to drinking regular soda again, and she said she needed to get new jeans and wanted some new shoes. She showed me a picture she had cut out from *Teen Vogue* magazine of a pair of baby-blue glitter and suede Skechers sneakers. I could never have pulled them off. Even Isabella Bowman couldn't have pulled them off, but they'd look perfect on Simone. Her mom dropped us off at the door and said she'd meet us for lunch at one o'clock in front of the giant hamburger statue. Simone suggested we head to Macy's first to look around and check everything out.

"I have to get a new backpack," she said. "My old one is gross."

She picked out a backpack with pink writing on it, but it was too expensive. She found a pink one she liked, but she worried it would be too cutesy with her hair color. Then she pulled out a baby-blue DKNY backpack, which was beautiful, but super small and meant to be used as a purse and not a school bag.

"Um, there's no way you'd be able to fit any

books into that," I said. "It's cute, but…"

Maybe you're right," she said, dumping it into the pile.

At Goodacre Academy, all the girls carried bags. Only the boys used backpacks. I tried on a purple one and it felt weird to have something over both shoulders. Simone shook her head at me and pushed one of the straps off my shoulder.

"You sling it over one side," she said. "Only kids wear it over both shoulders."

Simone decided to buy a light blue one and I bought the same one in purple. We tried on jeans next and I told her I wasn't allowed to wear them at my old school.

"I'd die if I couldn't wear jeans," she said. "I live in them."

I've always hated shopping for school clothes. I even used to avoid going to the grocery store once August started because seeing all those "Back to school" signs made me all queasy. I was so used to shopping with my mom for clothes, I didn't even know what size I wore. Simone had to turn down the back of my jeans to check the size for me. She headed to the Juicy Couture rack and picked out a bunch of stuff to try on, so I grabbed a few things and started to head into a dressing room.

"Wait," she said. "Let's get a big room and we can try on stuff together."

I felt kind of weird about changing in front of her, especially since Brittany Buchanan had made fun of my underwear. I had started wearing a better bra since then, but I truthfully didn't need to since I had nothing to fill it out. Simone didn't seem to mind and tossed her t-shirt in the corner. Of course, I had seen her in a bikini before which was kind of like underwear, so she didn't have anything to worry about. She pulled on a pair of jeans, tugged on a white turtleneck sweater and flipped her straight blonde hair out of the neck.

"Okay, yeah. I'm gonna get these," she said as she checked herself out from every angle. "Morgan always asks me if her butt looks big when she buys jeans. I always say she looks perfect even if they don't because it's not worth dealing with her crap."

"Morgan kind of looks good in everything anyway," I said.

Simone nodded. "Yeah, yet she'll purposely tell me and Asia we should buy something that doesn't look good on us. Like one time she told Asia to get a large sweater, when she was swimming in the bigger size. Asia looked way better in the fitted sweated, and it was like Morgan wanted her to look like a sack of potatoes. And she did the same thing with me—she told me I looked like I outgrew this sweater I tried on and made it seem like it looked too tight, but it fit perfect. I hate her mind games, you know?"

"I've only shopped with my best friend, Lexi, and she and I were always super honest about how we looked in stuff. I can't imagine trying to figure out if someone was telling me the wrong thing so they could look cuter than me—that's so weird."

"It's psycho," Simone said, glaring at her reflection in the mirror. "Do not tell her I said that though. Seriously, Hadley, even if you get super mad at me, don't ever tell Morgan I said that about her. Promise? Okay?"

"Promise."

I bought a red sweater and a pair of DKNY jeans. I was glad I found the jeans on the sale rack, because otherwise I would have spent all my money on them. We were heading to the shoe department when she grabbed my arm.

"Let's get some new makeup for school," she said.

We went over to the Cosmic Powders makeup counter and the clerk picked out a pink shimmer gloss for Simone and a blush-colored gloss for me. Simone told me she read Keri Ritchie had worn the same color in her latest movie. The woman said we got a gift with purchase if we spent eighteen-fifty. It seemed like a weird amount, especially since they didn't have anything which cost eighteen dollars and fifty cents. The lip gloss was thirteen dollars, so Simone bought an eyeliner pencil, and I bought some pink blush Simone swore Keri used too, so we could both get a free gift. As soon as we left the store, we went to sit down and look at our free stuff. There was a small bottle of perfume, a tube of raspberry lip stain, some mascara, something called "clarity serum," and a little jar of moisturizer.

"Don't tell my mom how much we spent," she said. "She'd freak out if she knew I spent so much on makeup. We're supposed to be on some stupid budget now 'cause I'm not working."

"Are you thinking about going back to acting?" I asked.

"Dunno. Hey, let's go to the bathroom to put on our new glosses before we meet my mom," she said, tugging my arm.

After lunch, Simone took me to a jewelry place and helped me pick out three pairs of earrings. I even found a pair that were like some Valeria owned. As I paid for my earrings, I noticed Simone was busy texting.

"So I have something to tell you and not sure how. I found out from Asia why Nick has been acting so weird and started dating that girl," she said.

"Why?"

"Remember I said Morgan likes to keep him as a backup?"

"Yeah, so? He's not going out with her."

"Well, apparently Morgan told him you had a boyfriend back in Goodacre and that she heard you talking to him on the phone at the Fourth of July party," Simone said.

"Oh man—the night we kissed?"

"Yup, Asia said he was super upset about it and called his ex after that. There is good news though," she said.

"How? How could there be good news? Unless you say his ex is going to live on the space station and has no plans to come back to earth anytime soon."

"Asia says he isn't super into that girl, her name is Reagan, and she thinks it's all some ego thing for him and it won't last," Simone said. "I'm really sorry, but it did backfire on Morgan with him asking that Reagan girl back out."

I shrugged and Simone told me that at least I could be assured it wasn't anything I did wrong, but it didn't hurt any less.

"Do you mind if we go home now?" I asked. "I'm not in a shopping mood anymore."

She nodded and put her arm around me.

***

Aunt Faith liked all the stuff I bought when I got home, but Grandma thought my jeans were too expensive, so I didn't tell her about the makeup. I hoped I'd fit in at my new school because I sure never felt like I fit in at my old one.

Chapter Eighteen

Grandpa and Dad had started painting our new house and they decided to tear up all the carpeting after Mom found a dead mouse in the kitchen. Dad made me promise not to tell Grandma about the mouse because he thought she'd completely freak out and lose it. I didn't mind staying at my grandparents' house, but Mom was going crazy. She said she liked Grandma Daniels, but she liked her a lot more when we lived two hours and forty-five minutes away from her.

"Excited about school tomorrow?" Aunt Faith asked me.

My stomach flip-flopped. "Um, no," I said. "More like terrified."

"You'll be fine. It's a small school, so not as intimidating as your old one. That's something, right?"

I nodded and went to call Simone to ask what I needed to bring on the first day.

"Make sure to bring lunch money, because only losers bring their lunch, and bring lip gloss and breath mints in case we get cute guys in our class, and a hair thingy in case your hair goes flat," she said.

"I meant like, school supplies."

"Oh, a notebook or some paper," she said. "I guess I'm gonna like, need a pen or something."

I called Charlotte, and she told me to bring a number two pencil, some erasable pens, a binder for math, a five-subject notebook, folders, a red pen, a ruler, and a box of tissues.

"And don't forget to bring your lunch," she said. "The cafeteria food is gross."

I didn't want to look like a loser, but I made a turkey sandwich to stick in my backpack in case the cafeteria was serving something weird. I packed my backpack and went to bed. I stared at the ceiling for hours. I was so nervous about starting the tenth grade. I mean, I got nervous at the start of each school year, but at least in Goodacre, I already knew those people. How would I do in a school where I only knew a couple of people? And what if Charlotte was wrong and they decided to split up the lunch periods? I'd die if I had to eat lunch in the bathroom again.

***

I was completely stressed out the next morning. Grandma made waffles, but I only ate a bite and I threw up from nerves right before Charlotte came over to pick me up. Mom talked to her while I brushed my teeth to get rid of the vomit taste. Mom had to go with me to make sure all my files from my old school had arrived. I'd asked Simone if she wanted a ride to school, but she was getting a ride from Asia's mother.

"I cannot wait until next year when we'll be allowed to drive to school," she said.

Mom pulled up to the school and I felt my stomach lurch again. I felt dumb going into school with my mother, but it was sort of nice to have her there. The secretary in the office said all my stuff had come in so Charlotte walked me to class. Simone was already sitting by the windows, so I sat behind her. She had worn an H&M jean skirt and a pink shirt with her straw sandals. I hadn't even realized we could wear sandals to school. I would have gotten sent home if I wore sandals at my old school.

Our teacher came in and I started to relax. Mrs. Feldman had short red hair, and she reminded me of the nurse at Goodacre Academy. The door opened as Mrs. Feldman read off our names.

"Oops, sorry I'm late," said a voice, and in walked Nick's new girlfriend looking runway flawless. Oh, kill me now. No, this was *not* happening.

Mrs. Feldman asked the girl what her name was, and she said Reagan O'Hara. Reagan walked over and sat right in front of Simone. Mrs. Feldman made us take a test to see what we had learned last year. I was finishing up a story problem when I heard Reagan whisper to Simone that she loved her sandals.

"Thanks, they're Steve Madden," Simone said.

"I know, see?" Reagan stuck her foot out into the aisle and she was wearing the same pair of strappy red sandals with a flower on the side. Meanwhile, I was wearing a pair of pink sneakers that made me look like I was going to playgroup or something. The bell rang and I leaned over to pick up my backpack. I got up and Simone and Reagan were walking out together. What was this? She was going to hang out with Reagan now?

I got lost looking for my English class and walked in late. The teacher glared at me over her glasses as I tried to find an empty seat. I ended up sitting behind Pilar and Morgan. The teacher, Mrs. Simpson, told us we were going to have free reading days every Friday. Pilar sighed, and she and Morgan exchanged a look. Pilar kept flipping her long black ponytail on my desk while I was trying to take notes. Her hair smelled like Herbal Essence shampoo. I met Charlotte and Deidre outside of the lunchroom when the bell rang. I went looking for Simone, but she was already in line with Asia. The cafeteria was serving chili and it smelled like body odor.

"Did you bring something?" Charlotte asked.

I nodded and followed them to a table. Deidre and Charlotte had almost every class together, but I only had one class with Charlotte. I saw Simone paying the cashier and I tried to get her attention. She didn't look up, and she and Asia went to sit with Morgan and Pilar. Then I saw Simone look up and start waving. I started to get up and then realized she was waving Reagan over, the girl she had only known for about five minutes and was my almost boyfriend's new girlfriend. Was there no loyalty anywhere?

I had social studies with Simone, so I saved her a seat. Simone walked into the room with Reagan and I motioned to her. Simone said she promised to sit with Reagan too.

"You want to sit with Nick's girlfriend?" I asked.

"From what I've heard, she doesn't even know he was ever talking to you. They broke up months ago and she went to Traverse City for a few weeks, and she came back *after* the whole Fourth of July party thing," Simone said. "See? She's totally innocent in all of this."

"How long did they date before?" I asked.

"Well…they were together last summer, I guess. She doesn't normally live here year round, so that's why I didn't know her. She's super sweet though."

Sweet? She didn't seem sweet to me. Although I guess I couldn't hate her for coming in between me and Nick since she technically hadn't, right?

"Well…maybe we can all sit together," I said, looking around for three empty seats together.

"Simone, over here," Reagan said, pointing to two empty seats on the other side of the room.

Simone said we could sit together in science class, which was next period. I nodded, but for now I was stuck sitting by myself. Maybe I could get to class early tomorrow and save seats for the three of us.

Our teacher, Ms. Crawford, passed out our textbooks and started writing on the board. I couldn't pay attention because I was watching Reagan and Simone whispering to each other. They had known each other for one day and were already acting like best friends. At least Simone remembered to wait for me after class.

"I heard Mr. Martin is tough," Simone said as we walked to the science room.

The room had little tables for two instead of regular desks. I stopped in the doorway and bit my lip.

"I'll sit at a table with Hadley, and Reagan, you sit behind us," Simone said.

I felt relief, but Reagan's lips formed a straight line and she looked like she wanted to say something.

"Okay, people. We need to pick lab partners—only work in groups of two, got it?" Mr. Martin said.

Reagan moved up to work with us, and I hoped that our little group of three would fly under Mr. Martin's radar. We were working on filling a bottle with vinegar and baking soda. Reagan and Simone were trying to get the balloon on the bottle when Mr. Martin came over.

"Girls, we have an uneven number here and I need one of you to work with Max Wright," he said.

I hoped Reagan would offer to go since Simone had agreed to sit with me, but she didn't say a word, and Mr. Martin asked me if I'd mind moving.

I didn't know what to say. I wanted to say Simone was my partner and I shouldn't have to leave, but I got up and moved to work with the short, funny-looking kid who smelled like ham and rubbing alcohol. I hoped he'd at least know what he was doing, but I had to do the whole lab by myself while he stared at his shoes. I could hear Reagan and Simone laughing on the other side of the room. Their balloon had blown up like it was supposed to, but ours had only sprayed foam on us. My brand new shirt was soaked with vinegar and it stunk. The bell rang, and I had to clean up by myself because Max had left.

Charlotte saved me a seat in our next class. We were working on the first chapter when my eraser fell out of my pen and I asked Charlotte if I could borrow hers. She took off her pen cap and I noticed the ring she was wearing. It was a pinky-peach color and made from a seashell.

"That's pretty. Where did you get the ring?" I asked.

"Deidre got it for me when she was on vacation," she said, twisting the ring on her finger. "She has one too."

Great, she and Deidre had matching rings, Simone had a fabulous new friend, and I had ham boy for a lab partner. This school year was already crappy and it was only the first day, which meant I still had to come back tomorrow. Ugh.

"Do you want to come over after school?" Charlotte asked. "Deidre and I are going to do our homework together."

"I guess," I said.

We went to Charlotte's house and all I heard about was how Deidre and Charlotte had all the same assignments since they had so many classes together. Oh, how precious. Gag. They worked together, and I had to do all my work by myself. I called Simone when I got back to my grandparents' house, but her mom said she was at Asia's house.

Next Door To A Star

Mrs. Hendrickson said she'd have Simone call me when she got home, but she never called me back.

Chapter Nineteen

Simone was already in class and talking to Reagan when I got there the next morning.

"I got your message, but I got home too late to call you," she said.

She started to say something else, but Reagan tapped her arm to get her attention. I wanted to see if I could eat lunch with her, but I was afraid to ask. Instead, I ate with Deidre and Charlotte, and they were telling me this funny story about their science class. It didn't seem funny to me, but I tried to laugh. I hurried to get to social studies so I could sit next to Simone, and I saved seats for both Simone and Reagan. They spent most of the hour whispering to each other and Simone barely spoke to me.

I was dreading science class and having to sit next to Max. He was already at our lab table, and he was wearing a pair of plaid shorts that made his legs look shorter and whiter than usual. We had another lab assignment, and Max broke a test tube. Mr. Martin said we'd have to stay after to finish the lab, but Max said he rode the bus home. So I was now stuck doing the whole thing. I banged my stuff on the desk when I got to my next class.

"What's the matter?" Charlotte asked.

"I have to stay after because my idiot lab partner messed up our project."

"Simone?"

"No, this guy named Max. Will you stay after with me?" I asked.

"I would, but I promised Deidre I'd go over to her house. You could come over when you're done," she said.

"When did she ask you to come over?"

"I dunno. This morning. Why?" she asked.

I shrugged and said, "No reason." Deidre could have asked me to come over when she saw me at lunch, but it was obvious she wanted Charlotte all to herself. I thought this year would be different, but maybe I wasn't meant to have friends.

***

Charlotte got sick the following week and was absent. I sat at our usual table at lunch, but Deidre went to sit with some other girls. She didn't even come over and ask me to join her. My face got hot, and I crumpled up my sandwich and went to the bathroom. I stayed in there until the bell rang and called Charlotte after school to see how she was feeling.

"I have pneumonia," she said. "It was my first chance to watch *Charmed Lives* since school started and I slept right through it."

"When do you think you'll be back at school?" I

asked.

"Not for a while."

"Wow, I hope you feel better. I can get your homework for you and drop it off."

"Don't worry about it. Deidre said she'll bring it home for me. She's in most of my classes anyway, so it's easier for her to get it."

I got off the phone and Grandma asked me what was wrong. I told her and she blew it off.

"Let the other girl bring her the homework. Why would you want to go over there and catch her germs?" she asked. "You're lucky you don't have to be exposed to pneumonia."

I wouldn't have minded getting sick and missing a few days of school. I thought this school year was going to be different because I had Charlotte and Simone, but I was still alone.

I went over to the new house and Dad had finished my room. The house smelled like sweat and paint, and I pulled my shirt over my nose when I went into my room. I wanted a yellow room and even picked out a soft yellow carpet, but we found a big stain on the wall when they removed the rooster wallpaper. They painted over it, but the stain still showed through the yellow paint. Aunt Faith knew I had my heart set on having the walls yellow, and she suggested we paint two of the walls a different color. Grandpa had some leftover lilac paint in his garage, so they painted both the stained wall and the wall across from it lilac. Grandma didn't like it, saying it, "Was like a cheap Easter egg." Aunt Faith reminded her it wasn't her room.

Simone told me she'd go with me to buy stuff for

my bedroom, but she was never home when I called. She was either with Morgan, Pilar, and Asia, or her new friend Reagan.

"Dad, when can we move my furniture in?" I asked.

"Not for a couple of days," he said. "How do you like the purple?"

It was pretty, but I still couldn't picture it as my bedroom. Also, I had unpacked my dollhouse, and Mom said I'd either have to store it in the garage and risk it getting moldy and bug infested in there, or I keep it in my room. I had outgrown it years ago, but I didn't like the idea of something that had once been so special to me sitting in a damp garage. I knew Charlotte would like it, but I didn't know if Simone would be coming over, and I didn't want her to think I was some immature kid. Maybe I could put it in the back of the closet.

Simone called when I came back to my grandparents' house and wanted me to come over. I asked Aunt Faith if I could, but she told me to wait until after dinner. I hoped Simone wouldn't call somebody else in the meantime.

"I'll come as soon as I'm finished eating," I said.

"Okay. Whatever," Simone said.

I sped through dinner and ran over to her house. Grandma was convinced I'd throw up before I reached her house, but my dinner stayed down. Simone said her mom was out on another date with "Bob, the giant loser." We went to her room and I noticed her bear, Glitter, was stuck underneath her blanket.

"Did you see the skirt Morgan was wearing

today?" she asked. "I'm surprised the principal didn't send her home."

I didn't think Morgan's skirt was too short, but I nodded.

"You know, Morgan asked Reagan to go shopping with her this weekend, and she didn't even invite Asia and me," she said.

"Is Pilar going too?" I asked.

"Of course, 'cause Morgan can't go anywhere without her shadow." She rolled her eyes. "Morgan's had an attitude problem lately."

I wanted to say, "Only lately," but I knew they'd eventually make up and didn't want to chance my comment getting back to Morgan.

We started playing with her makeup, and she told me she had taken the clarity serum from our free gift and used it on her eyelids.

"See? It gives a nice little shimmer," she said, closing her eyes. I put some on my eyes, but it made my lids look oily.

Simone wanted me to stay until her mom got home. Mrs. Hendrickson didn't get home until nine, and I ended up having to stay up late to finish my homework.

Chapter Twenty

Simone sat with me at lunch because Morgan was mad at her for copying her nail polish. Simone's polish was pale pink and I didn't see what was so unique about it. I asked if Pilar and Asia were mad at her too.

"No, but they kind of go along with whatever she says," she said.

Reagan came over and sat down across from Simone and started squirting a ketchup packet all over her fries. Reagan was wearing a jean skirt with a lilac top, which matched her lace up sandals. She seemed more like a model than a tenth grader. Simone had jeans and a t-shirt on like me, except hers were cuter, trendier, and made her look a lot older. I made a decision to wear some makeup other than lip gloss and blush tomorrow. Maybe Simone could show me how to put on eyeliner again or I could try the serum stuff on my lids. I was sick of looking younger than everybody else.

Simone wanted to know what Morgan had said when Reagan told her she was sitting with us. Reagan shrugged.

"Whatever, nobody tells me who I can and can't sit with," she said.

I could tell Simone was impressed, because nobody ever stood up to Morgan.

"Are you still going shopping with them tomorrow?" Simone asked.

"Yeah. Do you want me to talk to her or something?" Reagan asked.

"Nah, she'd get mad, but maybe we could do something tonight," Simone said.

"Oh, Pilar and I are spending the night at Morgan's." She shrugged. "Sorry."

I wished Simone would ask me to do something, but she went back to eating her lunch.

We walked back to class and Simone and Reagan passed notes all hour. I hoped Ms. Crawford would catch them and make Reagan move to another seat way across the room, but she never did.

Max wasn't in science class and Mr. Martin let me work with Simone and Reagan. Simone went to the bathroom and I tried to think of something to say to Reagan, but she had this way of making me feel like a little kid.

"I like your skirt," I said.

"Huh? Oh, thanks. My boyfriend loves when I wear it," she said, and my stomach flipped over. "Can you hand me the beaker?" she asked.

I went to pick up the beaker, but I knocked it over and water went everywhere. Fabulous, I had become Max Wright. I went to get some paper towels, which Reagan snatched from me to wipe her skirt.

"I'm so sorry," I said.

Next Door To A Star

"Do you know how much this cost? It's Topshop," she snapped. "Don't stand there, you moron, get some paper towels."

Simone came back and asked what happened. Reagan rolled her eyes as I wiped off the table. Reagan's notes were soaked, but all she cared about was her stupid skirt. The bell rang and I hurried to finish cleaning everything. I grabbed my backpack and rushed into the hall. I ran into Morgan and knocked her backpack strap off her shoulder.

"Watch where you're going, spaz," she said.

Asia and Pilar didn't say anything, and I put my head down and hurried to class.

***

I called Charlotte as soon as I got home, but she was asleep. Simone called and asked me to come over because her mom was going out with Bob again.

Can you show me how to put on eyeliner again?" I asked as I sat on the floor. She traced my eyes and started smudging the line with a cotton swab when the phone rang. It was Asia asking if Simone wanted to go to a movie tonight.

"Okay, do you want to meet at the theater?" Simone asked. I stared at my hands while they talked.

"Okay, we'll meet you in, like, ten minutes," she said and hung up the phone. "Hadley, do you want to call your mom and make sure you can go?"

"Go where?" I asked.

"To the movies. Duh. Don't you want to go?"

she asked.

I nodded and she went to change. I ran to my grandparents' house, but Aunt Faith was the only one there. She gave me some money for the movie and told me to call my dad for a ride home because she didn't want us walking home at night. Asia was waiting outside the theater for us.

The movie they wanted to see was rated "R" and I wasn't sure if they would sell me a ticket. Asia and Simone looked old enough to get in, but I wasn't so sure. However, the guy behind the counter didn't seem to care about age restrictions—either that or my new haircut did make me look older like Mom said. We got sodas and Simone sat between us.

The movie was kind of scary, and I had to look at the floor when the tree came to life and ate the kids. I noticed Asia had her head down too.

After the movie, we went to the pizza place. We ordered a medium pepperoni pizza and a pitcher of Coke. Simone went to the bathroom while Asia drained her soda.

"So that was pretty scary, huh?" I said.

"Hmm? Oh, the movie. Yeah," she said, using her straw to chip the ice at the bottom of her glass.

"It freaked me out when the tree came to life," I said.

"Oh my gosh. Yes, but I'm a wimp about those movies," she said. "I watched *Caboose of Horror* at Morgan's two weeks ago, and I'm still having nightmares."

She flipped her long brown hair over her shoulder and leaned on her arm. I felt like I was boring her and tried to come up with something else to say.

"I like your jeans," I said.

"Do you? For real?"

I nodded. "They're super cute."

She bit her lip. "Morgan told me they made my hips look wide. I only wore 'em because I'm bloated. Geez, why is it taking so long to make our pizza? There's nobody in here."

"Hey, Lucas is over there," I said.

"Where?"

"With the girl in the striped shirt. Does he have a new girlfriend?" I asked.

"Um, not according to Morgan," she said. "Oh man, he's got his arm around that chick too. Morgan would freak if she saw him."

"Are you gonna tell her?" I asked.

She widened her green eyes. "No way. She'd take it out on me like it was my fault or something. I'm going to pretend I didn't even see them."

"Hey, Asia," Lucas said as he walked out the door. Asia gave him a weak smile.

"Oh no, now if he tells her he saw me then she'll know I know about the other girl," she said. "This is a disaster."

"But what's he going to say? He saw you while he was out with another girl?" I asked.

"Good point. If she ever says anything, I can pretend I assumed he was with his cousin or something," she said. "I mean, for all we know that was his cousin...that he has a creepy relationship with."

"Pretend you didn't see the arm around the

shoulder thing," I said.

Simone came back to the table and we told her what had happened. She wasn't surprised Lucas was seeing someone else.

"I mean, he is a senior now," Simone said. "Was Connor with him?"

I shook my head. We devoured our pizza and Asia asked if we wanted to come over. Simone's mom wouldn't be home until twelve, and I called my parents from Asia's cell phone. Grandma answered the phone and asked me a million questions about where I was going.

"Who is this Asia? I've never heard you mention her name before. Did you only meet her tonight? She could be a crazy person—"

"She's in my grade. We're going to hang out at her house for a little while," I said.

"Hang out? What is hanging out anyway? Do you hang out of a window? What does it mean? Are you going to watch TV? Talk sense, Hadley," Grandma said.

I tried to answer her without looking like a dork in front of the girls. Where did she think we were going? To a strip club? I told Grandma we were going to watch TV to get her off my back. I hung up and we went to Asia's house.

"Hey, I'm home," she said as we walked through the door.

Asia's dad, Mr. Milanowski, was reading in the living room.

"Hey, girls," he said. "Asia, your mom went to bed with one of her headaches, so keep the noise down."

"Oh, okay. We'll be quiet. Oh, this is Hadley," she said. "She recently moved here."

Her dad got up and shook my hand. I had never had an adult shake my hand before. Most of the time they nodded and ignored me.

We went to Asia's bedroom where she had a huge canopy bed. Her room was all shades of pink and cream and it reminded me of my bedroom back home in Goodacre. Simone plopped down in the armchair and Asia sat on the bed, so I started to sit on the floor.

"You can sit up here, Hadley," Asia said, patting the bed.

I sat next to her and Simone started looking through magazines. Asia brought us some fruit juice. I was afraid to drink mine because I didn't want to spill it on her expensive bedspread. I had read enough issues of *Teen Vogue* to know it was a Teen Couture bedspread and it was expensive. Asia opened her walk-in closet and I saw something sitting on the floor in the back of it.

"You have a dollhouse," I said. "Can I see it?"

Asia moved it so I could see it better. It was a peach-colored Victorian style house with a green roof. There were four rooms and a cupola at the top. She even had a different kind of wallpaper in each of the rooms. There was a living room, a kitchen, a bedroom, and a nursery.

"I collect miniatures. See, I put the bathroom in the hallway because my grandparents bought me a tub and a toilet, and I don't know where else to put it," she said.

Simone came into the closet and knelt down next

to me.

"Asia, this is so cool," Simone said. "I didn't know you had this."

"I've had it forever. I used to leave it out, but Morgan thought it was dumb and immature, so I stuck it in here," she said. "But I've been collecting forever."

"What's this room up here?" Simone asked, pointing to the cupola.

"Sometimes it's the maid's room, and sometimes I put the toilet up there when I don't know what to do with it," she said.

"I have a dollhouse too," I said. "I'm not sure if I'm going to, you know, put it out or whatever."

"You should, but don't invite Morgan over," Asia said, making a face.

"Or Pilar," Simone said.

"You know, Pilar used to come over and play with it back when we were in middle school, until Morgan said we needed to grow up," Asia said.

We checked out her dollhouse for a while and then Asia's dad drove us home. I was surprised Asia had been so nice and easy to talk to. I always assumed she would be as snobby as Pilar and Morgan.

Chapter Twenty-One

Charlotte called me the next morning and I told her about going to Asia's house. Charlotte said she was going to come back to school on Monday.

"But I haven't finished all of my homework yet," she said. "I swear, all I wanted to do was sleep and watch crappy TV shows."

I offered to come over and help her, but Grandma started making wild hand gestures. Grandma wrote on a piece of paper how I shouldn't go over there because I'd come down with pneumonia. Charlotte said she'd be okay, but she might call me later and we hung up.

"Don't worry, Grandma. I'm not going over there, but Charlotte is coming back to school on Monday."

"Well, don't let her breathe on you," she said. "All you need is to get sick. Are you going over to your house today?"

I nodded. "Dad said they set up my bed last night."

Krysten Lindsay Hager

My parents had put my furniture in my room, but not where I wanted it. My dad moved the furniture where I wanted it and then went back to Grandma's to get the rest of my stuff. So I spent the afternoon putting everything away. I called Simone to see if she wanted to come over, but her mom said she was out with Asia.

Simone called after dinner and I asked if she wanted to see my new room.

"You're all moved in now?" she asked.

"Yeah, my parents even slept here last night. The house isn't finished, but my room is done," I said.

"Is it okay if Asia comes with me? She's over here," she said.

"Sure, no prob," I said and went to tell my parents I had people stopping by.

I could tell my mom was happy I had some friends coming over. Sadly, I knew she was thrilled I had some friends, period. The girls knocked on the door and I showed them the house and then we went into my room.

"I love this carpet." Simone took off her sandals and dug her toes into the carpeting. "Why is everyone so anti-carpet? It's nice and soft and squishy. Seriously? Those HGTV people have it wrong. Carpet is where it's at."

"I like how you did the walls different colors," Asia said, and I told her about the ugly rooster wallpaper that had been up.

"So where's your dollhouse?" Simone asked.

I said it was in my closet, but it wasn't set up yet. They wanted to see it, so I brought it out. Mine was bigger than Asia's, but my wallpaper and furniture wasn't as nice. They offered to help me set it up, and I took out the shoeboxes with the furniture. I never thought in a million years that I'd be spending a Saturday night putting my dollhouse together with Simone Hendrickson and Asia Milanowski.

"Look at this little red couch," Asia said. "I love this, and it even has a ruffle on the bottom."

"I like the tiny perfume bottles," Simone said.

Asia picked up the toilet. "Where does this go?"

I pointed to the hallway. "I know it's weird, but I always kept it next to the staircase," I said.

"They need to make a bathroom for these things," Asia said. "It's a privacy thing."

Simone opened the shoebox with the bedroom stuff in it. "Asia, look at this," she said. "She has a little dollhouse for the kid's room."

"How cute, and there's a crib. You know what?" Asia said. "I'm keeping mine out of the closet. I don't care what Morgan thinks."

"She's probably jealous," Simone said.

I was looking through a box for the dining room table when I pulled out my old American Girl doll.

"Oh my gosh, it's Rebecca! I have this doll too," Asia said. "I had the school set."

"I have the Caroline doll, but her hair looks like fried wheat because I put hair volumizer on it," Simone said.

We didn't have our TV and DVD player hooked up yet, but we made some popcorn and ate in my room. Grandma was over, and she gave us water to drink because she didn't want us to stain the new carpet.

"So I decided to go to my dad's wedding,"

Simone said.

"What changed your mind?" I asked.

She shrugged. "Dad called on Thursday and said he wants me to be there. He's going to pick me up from school and we're driving to Mackinaw City and taking the ferry from there. The worst thing is I still have to be a bridesmaid. I thought I was safe since I never tried on the dress, but Tina ordered one for me anyway. I hope it doesn't fit."

"It'll be okay," Asia said. "Maybe Tina will have a hot nephew or something."

"Dad texted me a picture of the dress and it's light blue with spaghetti straps. Tina said she was worried it might be too big on top for me." Simone rolled her eyes.

"She seriously said that? How rude," Asia said.

"I know, she never thinks before she speaks. She told me her sister is having a shower for her and gave me a card where she registered for gifts," Simone said. "Like I'm going to buy her something for marrying my dad."

"Kinda stupid. Whatever," Asia said.

"I know," she said. "The shower's tomorrow afternoon, but I said I couldn't go."

***

That night, I decided to sleep in my new room. The room still smelled like paint, and it felt like my bed was facing the wrong way, even though it was in the same position it was at my old house. I couldn't sleep, and then I realized I had forgotten my bear at Grandma's house. I tossed and rolled over, but everything was off. Even my pillow and mattress seemed lumpier than I remembered. My parents hadn't put my blinds up yet, and there was a shadow of a crooked branch on the wall. It was like the branches of the stupid people-eating tree in the movie. I got up to get a drink of water and the floor creaked underneath me.

"What are you doing up?"

I jumped and spilled the water down my nightshirt. "Mom, you scared the crap out of me."

"Don't say 'crap.' I hate that word. Now go back to bed. It's two in the morning," she said.

"I can't sleep. Can I go back to Grandma's? I know where they keep their extra key and I wouldn't have to even bother them—"

"You'd scare them to death if you snuck in the door in the middle of the night. Now go back to bed and close your eyes," she said.

I smirked. "Seriously, Mom. Fabulous advice. Why doesn't everyone who can't sleep try closing their eyes?"

She laughed and told me to get to bed.

Chapter Twenty-Two

Charlotte came back to school on Monday, and Deidre sat with us at lunch. Morgan had gotten over being mad at Simone and they were one big happy family again. I was having an okay day, and even science class went pretty well. Mr. Martin was making us do a mock research paper.

"Since this will be your first time writing a research paper, we're going to write about something you've all studied in the past—leaves. Think of this as a grown up version of a leaf collection—leaf collection 2.0, if you will," Mr. Martin said. "And now for the best part—you get to spend the whole hour outside looking for leaves."

Max followed me around like a lost dog. You could tell Reagan was making him nervous.

"Is he your boyfriend?" Reagan asked in a phony sing-songy voice.

His face went red and he walked away.

"Ah, no," I said.

"Too bad. You two would make a cute couple,"

she said. "They say like attracts like, after all."

If I had any guts at all I would have asked her what she meant by that comment, but I ignored her. I thought Simone would jump to my defense, but she was too busy picking out oak leaves. Did she even hear Reagan's stupid comment? I hoped not, because I wanted to believe she'd stand up for me, but I couldn't say for sure that she would.

Later, I saw Asia in the hall with Morgan and Pilar. Asia gave me a smile, but she didn't say anything. Things had changed now that we were back in school. Sometimes Simone didn't talk to me as much at school because she was busy with her cool friends. I guess I was only good enough to hang around with when Morgan was mad at her or her other friends weren't around.

***

Simone wasn't in school the next day. Her dad had decided to pick her up a day early to get ready for the wedding. Mr. Martin had us work on our leaf paper in class. I thought Reagan would work with me since Simone was absent, but she joined two other guys instead. Max didn't say anything to me as he went through the book for the information on his leaves. He had already collected all of his thirty leaves, but I only had fifteen. I saw Reagan flirting with one of the boys. What did Nick see in her?

We had a spelling bee in sixth hour, and I made it through the first few rounds. Only Charlotte, Byron Horowitz, and I were still standing. I thought I had a pretty good shot at winning because I had studied the vocabulary list last night. We had gone through the words from the first three chapters, and then our teacher decided to ask us to spell state names next. Charlotte got "Mississippi" and I breathed a sigh of relief. She got it right, but I would have freaked out from all of those "i's" and "s's." My turn was next and I got "Louisiana."

"L-O-U-I-S-A-I-N-A. Louisiana," I said.

"I'm sorry, incorrect. Byron, please spell 'Louisiana.'"

I was so embarrassed as I walked to my seat. It wasn't even worth getting so far if it meant I had to fail in front of all of those people. Nobody even noticed who had to sit down before, but now it was pretty obvious who failed when there were only three people standing up there. Charlotte and Byron kept going until the teacher decided to call it a tie and they both got candy bars as prizes. Charlotte offered to split hers with me, but it wasn't big enough to split. Why couldn't the whole, "let's give it to more than one person" thing come up when I was still standing up there? Next time, I was going to screw up on purpose in the beginning so I didn't have to get humiliated later.

Chapter Twenty-Three

I didn't see Simone until Monday morning.

"How was the wedding?" I asked.

She rolled her eyes and said, "Don't ask."

Later, I overheard her telling Reagan about having to dance with some "loser-dork" guy from the wedding party. At lunch, I ran into Asia.

"Hey, Hadley. How are your classes going?" she asked.

I was surprised she asked, but she was by herself, so I guess it was okay to talk to me.

In science, Simone told me to come over tonight so we could work on our leaf papers. It had rained all weekend so I didn't get the chance to go out and collect more leaves.

I went to her house at four o'clock and her mom said she had left with Morgan and Pilar. I was confused because she had told me to come over at four, but I guess I wasn't as important as her other friends. I walked over to Charlotte's house and told her Simone had basically stood me up.

"I can't believe her. Well, she's flighty, so maybe she forgot or double booked. I'll help you," Char said. "Grandpa, we're going out for a walk," she said as she pulled on her jacket. "Hadley needs leaves for her research paper."

"You can get some leaves in the yard, but no going into the woods," he said. "You're only starting to feel better and it's too cold for you to be out too long."

We went around her yard, but I only found three leaves I didn't have already. My project was due Wednesday, and I had to classify them and then iron them between pieces of wax paper.

Charlotte gave me a book she had gotten from the nature center and I asked my grandpa if he'd help me look for leaves after dinner. We went out for a bit, but it got dark pretty fast. He promised he'd help me tomorrow, but I felt like I'd never find enough leaves and get it finished by Wednesday.

***

Simone wasn't in first hour on Tuesday. I got to science class early and finished classifying the leaves I was able to find. Reagan walked by my table and knocked Max's project on the floor with her butt. I didn't know if she did it on purpose, but I picked it up for him.

"Thanks. Did you get all thirty?" Max asked.

"Not yet," I said.

"I have extras if you want 'em," he said, staring at his hands.

"Seriously? Thanks. Which ones do you have?" I

asked.

He showed me a bunch of leaves and they were all ones I could use. Now I only needed two additional leaves and I'd be done. Simone came up to me after class.

"Do you want to work on the project after school?" she asked.

"I thought we were supposed to meet yesterday," I said.

"Yeah, sorry. Yesterday was crazy," she said, brushing her bangs out of her face. "So what time do you want to get together?"

"I can't. I have to do something with my grandpa. Maybe Reagan can help you," I said.

"Reagan? She hasn't even started hers yet," she said. "Well, call me if you guys get back early, okay?"

"Okay," I said and walked over to meet Charlotte.

Grandpa and I went for a walk and I found the two additional leaves I needed to complete my collection. Grandma ironed my leaves for me since she was convinced I'd burn my hands off if I did it myself. To be honest, she was probably right. I had never ironed anything other than my hair with a straightening iron, and even then I burned myself five times.

Simone called during dinner to see if I was back yet.

"Do you have any extra leaves?" she asked. "I'm missing seven."

"I only have a maple leaf left. Do you have one of those?"

"Yeah. Shoot, my mom's working late and I think our iron's broken or something," she said.

"Do you want to use our iron?"

"Could I? That would be awesome. I'll come over as soon as I get to the ironing part. You are the best, Hadley. The best!"

Simone showed up at my grandma's house at nine o'clock, and I was already finished with my project. Simone was still three leaves short and she didn't even have all of her information completed.

"Can I see yours? You know, for help?" she asked.

Help? Or to copy down all my info instead of taking the time to look it up on her own? Whatever. "All the information is in the book," I said.

"I know, but it takes, like, forever to look each one up," she said. "This project is so dumb. It's basically like we're doing a little kid leaf collection and not a real research paper."

I wanted to say, that was the whole point—it was a mock research paper to get us ready to write a real one, but she would have had to be paying attention to the teacher to get that. Instead, I said my book was in my room, and she assumed I meant it was at the other house. It was upstairs, but I didn't think it was fair for her to copy my information when I had to look up all the stuff on my own—especially since she had ditched me yesterday to hang out with her friends. Grandma finished ironing her leaves and Simone went home.

***

I got to science class early the next day to hand in my leaf research paper. Mr. Martin flipped through it and nodded with approval. I thanked Max again for the leaves. Reagan wasn't in class, but she had been in my first hour and at lunch. I wondered if she finished her paper. We were working with microscopes to examine the parts of a leaf and Simone pulled up the stool next to me.

"Hi, guys," she said. Max stared at his feet as I tried to get the leaf in focus. I asked her if she got the rest of the leaves after she left Grandma's house.

"I was short two leaves," she said. "Oh well."

"Where's Reagan?" I asked.

"She wasn't feeling well at lunch."

Funny, since I saw her at lunch with a tray full of ice cream and spaghetti. She seemed perfectly healthy then. Perhaps it was something about having a major paper due that made her feel so sickly.

Mr. Martin told us to add a drop of iodine to the leaf on the slide. Max reached for the bottle and he wound up spilling it on Simone's notebook.

"Idiot," she said, grabbing her sopping notebook.

"Simone, it was an accident. You don't have to call him names," I said. She stared at me and then got up to get some paper towels.

"Thanks," Max said. "It sort of slipped."

Normally, I'd be irritated with Max too if he spilled something on my stuff, but at least he came through for me when I needed help, unlike a certain blonde who only ran to me when her cool friends were too busy.

Simone came back and wiped up her notebook.

Mr. Martin told her she could recopy her lab partner's notes to make up for the ones that had smeared. I wanted to laugh. Fat chance. The only thing Reagan ever wrote down was a list of makeup to buy, or when she made a list of cute actors and ranked them in order of cutest appearance. It made me sick wondering what Nick saw in her. She was mean, passive aggressive, and superficial.

Simone always did the labs by herself while Reagan watched. At least I would have helped if I had been Simone's lab partner.

Charlotte had a doctor's appointment and left early during class. I was walking home by myself when Simone ran up to walk with me. I figured she wanted to borrow my science notes, but she asked if I wanted to do something. I didn't have any homework, so we went to her house. She grabbed a bag of chips from the kitchen and we went to her room. I saw her bridesmaid's dress hanging in plastic on the back of her closet door.

"Can I see it?" I asked.

She wrinkled her nose but lifted the plastic up. The dress was made of icy-blue satin and it had a long skirt. She said the top had been too big and Tina's mom had to sew little pads into the front.

"Did you have fun?" I asked.

"No, one of Tina's relatives asked her who I was and she said, 'Oh, just Simone.' Not 'Peter's daughter,' or 'my stepdaughter', but 'just Simone,'" she said. "Although, I guess I would have puked if she called me her stepdaughter."

She said Tina kept saying she wanted to have a big family. I thought Simone was going to cry. She pulled the plastic back over the dress and shoved it into the back of the closet. Then she pulled out her hair clip and started twisting her hair up in a bun.

"If my grandma was still alive she wouldn't even like Tina. She'd say Tina was fake and super annoying, but now Tina's talking about naming a baby after her," she said, twisting her hair. "You know, my mom was supposed to have a boy. Jacob Peter."

I didn't know what to say, so I stared around the room. I noticed she had put her Caroline American Girl doll in the hanging wicker chair. The doll's hair was a mess, and someone had put eyeliner on her.

"I have today's episode of *Charmed Lives* on my DVR. Wanna watch?" she asked.

We went into the living room and watched TV until Mom called me home for dinner.

Chapter Twenty-Four

Simone was late to class the next day. She didn't look at Reagan or me when she sat down and she shot up out of her chair and left as soon as the bell rang. Later, I saw her sitting with Morgan and Reagan at lunch when I was in the lunch line. Asia was in line in front of me and she asked if I knew what was bothering Simone. I shrugged.

"Her step-mom isn't pregnant or anything, is she?" she asked.

"I don't think so," I said.

Pilar walked by and asked Asia to buy her a brownie as she went to sit down. I said I was dying for a brownie too, but there was only one left when we got to the tray.

"Take it," Asia said.

"Are you sure?" I asked.

"Yeah, it's fine," she said. "I'll tell her they were out."

Next Door To A Star

***

We had a test in science, so I couldn't talk to Simone in class. Mr. Martin said we could go to the library when we were finished with the exam, but Simone wasn't in there. I asked the librarian for a pass and went to the bathroom. I walked in and heard somebody crying in one of the stalls. I recognized the Steve Madden shoes under the handicapped stall door.

"Simone?"

"Go away."

"Are you okay?" I asked.

"I'm fine. Leave me alone," she said.

"I'll give you my Jack Brogger sticker if you let me in," I said.

"I don't like him anymore," she said.

"How about my Josh Haven folder?"

"Loser, you don't even have one," she said, but she pushed the door open. She was sitting on the floor, and her eyes were red-rimmed and her lips were puffy.

I sat on the floor next to her and she told me her dad called.

"What did he say?" I asked.

"He said Tina's pregnant and they've decided to move further away. Tina wants to live closer to her parents because of the baby, and now they're moving four hours away to St. Clair Shores. I barely see him as it is, but now he's gonna have his new family and I'm the leftover kid. I'm like the green thingy they put on plates at restaurants that you don't need. No one would even notice if they stopped putting it on the plates." Simone wiped her nose on her Forever 21 sweatshirt sleeve.

"Have you talked to him about it?" I asked. "You know, told him how you feel about everything going on?"

"About what? He thinks it's great. A new house, a new baby, and now free babysitting," she said. "Tina's mom seems like a real pain in the butt, and I hope she's over there all the time driving him nuts."

I reached up and got her a piece of toilet paper to wipe her nose.

"One of the reasons we left L.A. was because my parents were fighting all the time. I overheard my mom on the phone one day saying their marriage counselor thought my career was causing problems. I guess my dad was mad Mom was spending all her time on the set with me, so then he started being the one to stay with me, and then there was this weirdness when my mom found out one of the production assistants on the show had been sending my dad texts." She paused to blow her nose. "They got into a fight about it and he said my mom was always putting my career first."

"Is that why you left the show?" I asked.

"Not exactly. That whole texting thing was the main reason they started fighting, but the show…the producers were talking about recasting me with an older girl. I found out about it on accident. They brought this girl in and said she was a guest star, but she looked a lot like me, but with breast implants and stuff. I mean, this girl could have been my older sister, and I had a bad feeling the moment she walked on the set."

Next Door To A Star

"Are you sure they weren't going to have her play your older sister or something?" I asked.

"No, my agent found out they wanted to go with a 'sexier, older Abby,' but the girl had issues getting her lines memorized. They sort of put it out there that if I was willing to make myself look more like that girl, then I could keep the role."

"I don't understand," I said.

"My agent asked me what I thought about getting my boobs done," she said.

"Oh, wow. What did you say?"

Simone shifted. "I was terrified of losing my spot on the show, so I asked my mom if I could have the surgery done and she flipped."

"I don't blame her."

"Mom said between that girl who kept texting and calling my dad, and then the plastic surgery thing, that the whole TV scene wasn't healthy for any of us," she said. "So they told me I couldn't get the surgery. I was so mad, I like, cried my butt off. I thought it would make everything better."

"So you didn't want to leave the show?"

"No, of course not, but when I told my agent I wasn't going to have anything done, the show said that my character had run its course and they were writing me out. And right after I left, guess who came on the show? That older, sexy brunette who plays the long lost cousin. That girl's thirty-two and playing a sixteen-year-old. How can I compete with that? Anyway, then we moved and my mom lost the baby and they split up for good. I dunno, everything stinks. I have no career and now I have no father."

The bell rang and we both stood up.

"How bad do I look?" she asked.

I gave her a wet paper towel and she wiped the mascara that had smeared under her eyes.

***

After school, I saw Simone walking with Morgan, Asia, and Pilar. She was staring at the ground, but Asia waved to me as I went to meet Charlotte. It was pouring outside and Mr. Lidstrom was outside waiting for us in his car.

"Ladies, want a ride?" he called and we got in the backseat.

Simone called me later during dinner. Mom told me to call her back after we were done eating, but Aunt Faith said it sounded like she was crying. I got on the phone.

"You are not going to believe this," Simone said. "I told the girls about my dad moving, and Morgan told me not to be such a baby."

"Yikes," I said. "Well, Asia seemed worried—"

"Asia was nice about it, but why would anybody be such a jerk when it's obvious their friend is upset? I mean, what is Morgan's problem?"

"Did you get mad at her?" I asked.

"No. I didn't say anything, and Morgan thinks it was the end of it. I'm so sick of her," she said.

I gave Simone my Jack Brogger sticker the next day to make her feel better. She put it on her binder and Reagan saw it when she came in.

"You like this loser?" Reagan asked, peeling off the sticker.

"Don't. He's cute," Simone said, smoothing the

Next Door To A Star

sticker out.

We had Friday reading and I brought one of Charlotte's Jane Austen books. Pilar was in front of me and she kept flipping her ponytail and moving around until Mrs. Simpson told her to sit still and read her book. She sighed, opened her book, and folded back the cover. I couldn't even concentrate on my book because her ponytail kept moving across my desk like a snake. I started to get into the story when the bell rang. I saw Pilar close her book and realized she had stayed on page one the entire period.

Friday was pizza day and everyone always rushes to the cafeteria because they tend to run out of pizza, and the people at the end of the line get stuck with leftovers. I got in line in front of Morgan, Simone, and Asia. The cafeteria lady put the last slice of pepperoni and sausage on the counter, and Morgan and I reached for it at the same time. I would have let her have it, but it was the last piece and I got there first.

"Excuse me, this is mine," she said, tugging at the paper plate.

"No, it's mine."

"Morgan, she got it first," Simone said. "Give it to her."

Morgan yanked the plate away and the pizza hit my leg and landed on the floor.

"Look what you did you, you idiot," Morgan said. "There's sauce all over my shoes."

"You pulled it away from Hadley," Simone said to her.

"Is it 'Adopt a Loser Day' or something?"

Morgan said, turning to look at Simone as she wiped sauce off her shoes.

"Oh, shut up," Simone said, and the cafeteria lady told us to move along. I grabbed a peanut butter sandwich and hurried through the line. Simone and Morgan were still standing there and arguing. One of the cafeteria workers went and walked both of them out of the cafeteria.

Asia came over and handed me some napkins. I stared at her.

"For your jeans," she said.

I looked down and realized my upper leg had grease and sauce all over it. Charlotte let me borrow her sweatpants from gym class since mine were all gross. Charlotte and Deidre walked me to science class, but Simone wasn't there. Mr. Martin handed me my paper when I sat down.

"What did you get?" Max asked.

I flipped to the last page. I told him I got an "A" and he said he got an "A" too. I noticed he actually got an "A+," but it was nice he didn't brag about it.

Simone came into the room and nodded at me. I mouthed, "What happened?" and she shrugged. I waited for her after class and she said Morgan had gotten in trouble for taking my lunch.

"Did you get in trouble?" I asked.

"No, the cafeteria lady said I was sticking up for you. Morgan may kill me though," she said. "Wait for me after school. I might need a bodyguard."

***

Charlotte and I waited for Simone after school.

We were walking out when Asia ran out after us.

"Is Morgan super mad?" Simone asked her.

"She was over by her locker, but I didn't stick around to listen to her complain," Asia said. "Pilar was with her though. Poor girl, she'll have to hear about it the whole way home."

"Yeah, well, Reagan acted like she wasn't sure if she was supposed to talk to me or not," Simone said. "Some loyalty, right?"

I thought about how Simone was so quick to befriend Reagan and look the other way when she made passive aggressive remarks to me, but instead I asked Simone what she got on her paper.

She flipped to the back. "B+."

Charlotte was coming over to my house and I asked Simone and Asia if they wanted to come over too. I was afraid they might say, "Just because we were nice to you today doesn't mean we're all going to hang out now," but they said they'd come over. We went to my room and Asia knelt in front of the dollhouse.

"You put the sink in the baby's room," she said. "I'm moving it back into the hall—your original bathroom."

"I rolled up a pair of old tights to use as the blanket in the crib," I said. "It looks like a Teen Couture bed spread.

"Oh yeah. I love that brand too. The red hearts on the tights match the room. How cute. I should do it for my nursery," she said.

"You have a dollhouse too?" Charlotte asked her.

Asia nodded and described it to her. Mom got us

some chips and sodas and we sat eating Pringles on the floor.

"You guys, Morgan is seriously going to have me killed on Monday," Simone said.

"She'll get over it…after a while," Asia said.

"I was so mad at her when she told me not to be a baby about my dad moving," Simone said, looking at me. "You knew how upset I was, but Morgan didn't care."

Asia nodded. "Because it doesn't concern her."

I thanked Simone for sticking up for me as she was leaving.

She shrugged. "Well, you have to stick up for your friends, you know?"

I felt guilty since I hadn't for Charlotte when Morgan made fun of her.

I went back to my room. "Hey, Char? Do you want to spend the night?" I asked. She nodded and she called Mr. Lidstrom after my parents said it was okay.

I started telling her all about my old school and Brittany Buchanan while we got ready for bed. Charlotte said she used to be good friends with Morgan when they were in the fourth grade.

"You're kidding. What happened?" I asked.

She shrugged. "Pilar moved here and Morgan didn't like me anymore. It hurt when Morgan stopped talking to me. Then Asia moved here and Morgan dropped Pilar for a minute—"

"And then Simone moved here," I said.

"My grandpa always says you have to be a friend to have a friend," she said.

We stayed up late talking and didn't get to sleep

until after three o'clock in the morning.

Chapter Twenty-Five

On Monday, Reagan didn't talk to Simone in class. I saw Simone and Asia sitting together when I got to lunch. I started to head toward Charlotte and Deidre's table when Simone asked me to sit with them. Reagan was sitting with Morgan and Pilar, who were acting like she was their new best friend.

Morgan didn't talk to Simone for a few days, but she was at Simone's locker on Friday morning. They didn't seem to be arguing, and I knew they made up when Reagan started talking to Simone in class. Mrs. Feldman told us to pick partners for an assignment and Reagan asked Simone to be her partner.

"I already promised Hadley," Simone said.

Simone put her back to Reagan and moved her chair around to face my desk. Reagan seemed surprised and got up to look for a partner. I pulled out my book and we started working on the assignment.

"Reagan's so two-faced," Simone whispered.

Next Door To A Star

"She acted like she was sticking up for me with Morgan, but she's been talking about me behind my back."

"What are you going to do about it?" I asked, and she shrugged.

"It's hard to completely stop being friends with someone when there are only fifty kids in the entire tenth grade," she said.

Morgan hadn't even glanced at me since the pizza incident. She had always ignored me in English class, but on Wednesday she knocked my binder on the floor. It seemed like an accident, but there was no such thing as an accident when it came to Morgan Kemp.

Later, Simone and Asia came to sit with us during lunch.

"I thought you guys made up with Morgan," I said.

"We did, but I'd rather sit here," Simone said. "Actually, I'd rather sit in a pit of snakes. Wait, I wasn't calling you guys—never mind. You know what I was getting at."

I glanced over at Morgan's table and she was staring at us. She leaned over and whispered something to Reagan and they both started laughing.

"Looks like Morgan's got a new shadow," Asia said.

"What about Pilar?" I asked.

"Morgan gets sick of somebody and then she moves on," Simone said, taking a sip of her juice. "And sometimes she gets bored with her new friend and goes back."

"Yeah, best friends to the end," Asia said, rolling her eyes.

I glanced back at Morgan's table. Morgan and Reagan had their heads bent together and they were cracking up. Pilar was laughing, but she looked left out, and then Morgan handed her some money and Pilar got up to buy her something. The three of them were so gorgeous and grown up, like they were at least seventeen. I went back to my table and Charlotte was wiping grape jelly off her teddy bear sweatshirt. Simone started giggling.

"Sorry, I'm such a pig," Charlotte said, her face turning red with embarrassment.

"Don't make fun of her, Simone. You should talk, you have a little fruit punch mustache," I said.

Simone clapped her hand over her mouth and went in her backpack for her compact. She held up the mirror and realized I had been making it up.

"Loser," she said, punching me in the arm. "I wasn't making fun of her. Anyway, Charlotte, I have a hoodie you can borrow."

"Okay, thanks," Charlotte said.

***

On Friday, Morgan was waiting at Asia's locker after school. She asked Asia if she wanted to come over because Reagan was going to teach them how to do yoga.

"Reagan used to take yoga classes when she lived in Denver," Morgan said.

"Um, it sounds like fun, but I promised Simone I'd go over to her house," Asia said.

"You can go to her house anytime," Morgan said, bumping her playfully with her hip. "Come on, I never get to see you anymore. You're always with Simone."

"Well, we could hang out tomorrow or—"

"Why not today? Tell Simone you forgot you already had plans with me." Morgan grabbed Asia's arm. "Please? I want you to come over."

Asia bit her lip and told Morgan she had already promised Simone, but the two of them could do something tomorrow after school. Morgan's tone changed.

"Asia, Simone is using you because she has nowhere else to run to when I'm mad at her. She's, like, afraid of me now. It's so funny," Morgan said. "Tell her you can't go. Besides, you could use a little toning."

"Yeah, I gotta go. See ya," Asia said as she walked over to me.

Morgan went over to meet Reagan and we watched Pilar run to catch up with them.

"Don't you want to learn yoga?" I asked Asia.

"Maybe, but not because Morgan thinks I need it," she said. "I can't believe her sometimes. She makes me feel like I'm abandoning her and then she turns on me. She wanted me to cancel on Simone so she could have power over me. And that toning comment—seriously? How rude was that?"

We walked over to Simone's locker. I was supposed to meet Charlotte outside because we were going to the apple orchard today. Simone asked if I wanted to go shopping downtown with them. I wanted to go with them, but all Charlotte had talked about for days was apple cider, stuffing herself with donuts, and going for a hayride at the orchard. She had even taken a new allergy medication so she could be around all the hay.

"Nah, you guys go ahead. I'm going to the apple orchard with Charlotte. Have fun," I said.

"Don't eat too many donuts or you'll have to do extra yoga tomorrow," Asia said, tossing her hair like Morgan.

"I'll eat one for you," I said.

"Hey, text Asia's cell phone later," Simone said, writing the number on my hand. "Maybe we can all meet up and get ice cream or something. Ask Charlotte to come too."

Charlotte was sitting on the curb when I got outside. "I thought you forgot," she said, standing up.

"No way." I linked my arm with hers. "I wouldn't miss this for anything."

"Good. Because my new allergy pill only gives me ten hours, which means, like, four hours in normal allergy time."

We walked to Mr. Lidstrom's car and headed to the orchard. We picked a bunch of apples and then got donuts and cider. Charlotte and I ate the powdered sugar donuts, but her grandpa liked the plain kind. He dipped them in his coffee. There was a bunch of stuff for kids to play on there like bridges, rope swings, and this pulley thing you grab onto and it carries you out. I thought I was too old to play on stuff, but Charlotte wanted to try everything.

At first I felt stupid, but then I got into it and I

even tried the rope swing. I fell off, but I landed in a hay bundle, so it didn't hurt. On the way home, Charlotte asked me if I wanted to order a pizza for dinner. I told her Simone wanted me to call her after we got back.

"Oh, I didn't know you had plans with her," Charlotte said, biting her lip.

"She thought we could meet up," I said.

"Okay. Well, have fun," she said.

"No, she wants you to come too," I said.

Charlotte paused. "Are you sure I'm included?"

I nodded, but she didn't look convinced.

"We don't have to go if you don't want to." I didn't want to admit it, but I was a little worried Simone and Asia would run into Morgan and change their minds about wanting to hang out with us. I mean, if I was Simone I'd rather hang out with Pilar, Morgan, and Reagan than with Charlotte and me. I hoped things would be different this time and Simone wouldn't take me for granted anymore, but I couldn't count on it. I called Asia's cell phone and she said they were heading down to the boardwalk.

"Did you eat yet? We could meet at Fricano's Pizza Tavern for dinner and then get ice cream at Scoops," she said.

Charlotte's grandpa dropped us off at Fricano's and we waited for Simone and Asia. I was afraid they had changed their minds about meeting us, but they showed up ten minutes later.

"Sorry guys, I was trying on clothes," Simone said. "Look at this t-shirt I got."

We had planned to have pizza, but Asia saw Reagan sitting by the window with Nick.

Simone looked at me and I tried to pretend it didn't bother me.

"We could get hot dogs instead," Simone said. "And let's get them to go so we can sit by the water and eat since it's pretty warm out."

I smiled. "Thanks. That sounds better than watching…them."

Charlotte got two hot dogs with everything on them and a large root beer float. Simone was going to get a bunless hot dog and a diet root beer, but she changed her mind and got a corn dog and a root beer float instead. I tried to signal Charlotte to wipe her mouth because she was getting relish everywhere, but she ignored me. I handed her a napkin and she got the message. However, she also burped. Simone tried to hide her smile, but Charlotte looked like she was about to die of embarrassment.

"Excuse me," Char said.

"Root beer makes me burp too," Asia said. "You guys, eat some of my curly fries. I'll never finish 'em."

I never thought I'd be sharing fries with Asia Milanowski in a million years or sitting across a picnic table from a TV star. It was crazy that this was my life now. Simone thought she spotted Connor, but it wasn't him.

"You know, I tried e-mailing him, but he hasn't been returning my messages. He thinks he's so cool because he's a senior," she said.

"Don't worry about it," Asia said. "He told Pilar she was too young for him, but they were going out, like, a month ago. Lame."

"Things are different when you become a senior, I guess," Simone said, tracing circles in her ketchup.

We were going to walk downtown for ice cream, but Charlotte said they had homemade ice cream next door. We all got big waffle cones of chocolate chip cookie dough ice cream and walked down the boardwalk. There was a hole in the bottom of Charlotte's cone and the ice cream kept dripping out. She lifted the bottom of her cone to her lips and sucked out the melted ice cream. I was super embarrassed when Simone glanced over at her, but she didn't say anything. We walked down to the pier and Simone and Asia sat on the edge.

There were a lot of high school girls there and Simone and Asia seemed to fit right in, while Charlotte and I were like little kids. I wished I hadn't brought my Snoopy sweatshirt, but it was the first one I grabbed when I left. It was getting cool by the water as the sun was starting to go down, and it wasn't like I couldn't put it on unless I wanted to freeze. Meanwhile, Simone had on her favorite baby-blue Forever 21 hoodie, and Asia had gray and pink H&M sweats on. Char's and my sweatshirt both looked big and bulky, but Asia and Simone's were fitted. They might have been cold, but they were still cute.

"You guys, I'm freezing. Do you want to come over to my house?" Charlotte asked. "We could watch a movie or something?"

I thought Simone and Asia would say they'd had enough of the "kid show" and leave us to do something fun, but they agreed. Asia wanted to stop first at the newsstand to see if the new issue of *Teen Vogue* was out. Simone picked up the *Soap Opera Digest* with Valeria on the cover.

"Valeria has shorter bangs again," she said. "I wonder if I should do that too."

We picked up a Josh Haven movie and went to Charlotte's house. Mr. Lidstrom made us hot chocolate with whipped cream and put out some Rice Krispie treats for us. I was afraid Simone might think it was babyish, but she took one.

"I love Rice Krispie treats," she said.

Mr. Lidstrom didn't seem to know whether or not he should sit in the family room with us, so he hovered between the family room and the kitchen. He saw Simone's magazine and mentioned he read Valeria was dating a diplomat's son. Simone's eyes widened. Mr. Lidstrom showed her the article in one of his tabloids.

"You guys, listen to this," she said. "Valeria and the girl who plays Madison are best friends in real life. Look, they even go shopping together."

Charlotte sat up. "Are there any pictures of Lance Cunningham in there?"

"Yup, and I heard he and Madison dated in real life," Asia said.

"You're kidding," Mr. Lidstrom said. "I thought he was dating the girl who I think is going to be his sister-what's-her-face…Leocadia."

"I think they're going to find out they're brother and sister too," Simone said.

"My grandpa also thinks so," I said.

Asia started telling us about how Lance was known to date all his co-stars, and even Mr.

Lidstrom sat down to listen. I thought it was kind of funny Simone and Asia would have the same interests as a seventy-something-year-old man. Mr. Lidstrom got up to leave when Charlotte put the movie on, but Simone told him to watch it with us. Later, when we were walking home, Simone said she wished her grandfather were still alive.

"He passed away a couple of years ago," she said. "But we were close."

"Was he your mom's dad or your father's?"

"My mom's. My Grandpa Hendrickson is still alive, but I don't get to see him much. He stopped driving so he doesn't come to visit and we almost never go there."

She said her grandpa was supposed to go to her dad's wedding, but her grandpa got bronchitis so he couldn't come.

"Maybe you could call him," I said.

She shrugged. "I guess. He lives in Rockford now. He got remarried after my grandma died and I don't like his new wife. She's always telling me not to put my feet on the couch or where to set my drink. I feel like I'm in a museum when I'm over there…but maybe I will call and see how he's doing."

Chapter Twenty-Six

The next morning, Aunt Faith said she was going to drive to Saugatuck for an art festival. She asked my mom and me to go with her and said I could bring a friend. I called Charlotte first, but she was having allergy problems and she didn't want to be outside all day. I called Simone next, but she was in the car with her mom on their way to South Haven.

"Going to Saugatuck sounds like more fun," she said. "I wish I could go with you. Is Charlotte going?"

I told her Charlotte wasn't feeling well. I didn't want to say she had allergy problems because it sounded kind of dorky.

"Why don't you see if Asia can go?" she said.

I felt weird calling Asia, but I had been over to her house. Mainly, I was afraid she'd think I was a loser for thinking she'd want to do anything with me. I decided to call her after I overheard my aunt telling my mom how she wanted to visit the art galleries. It sounded like a boring trip, so I took a deep breath and called Asia's house.

"Hi, Asia. It's Hadley. If you're not doing anything today, uh, do you want to go to Saugatuck with me and my mom and aunt?"

"Sure! I love Saugatuck. What time should I be ready?"

"We could pick you up in an hour if it's okay. You know it's only me, my mom, and my aunt going, right?" I asked. I didn't want her to be disappointed Simone wasn't going to be there.

"Yeah, it sounds great. I'll bring some magazines for us to read in the car. See ya," she said.

I ran downstairs to tell my mom Asia was going. Grandma couldn't understand why I was so excited.

"Calm down," Grandma said. "Why wouldn't she want to go? Saugatuck is a fun place to be."

But my mom understood why I was so happy. Back in Goodacre, if I invited Lexi somewhere and she couldn't go, then I had no one else to ask. I wouldn't even have dreamed about calling someone like Asia a few months ago—not to mention inviting her somewhere. I was almost singing as I washed my hair. I had finished drying my hair when Mom said Asia was on the phone. Oh no. She was canceling. She probably got invited somewhere better...or by someone better.

"Hello?" I said as my mother watched me.

"I'm having a breakdown—"

"Oh, I understand if you can't go," I said.

"No, I can go, but I don't know what to wear. What are you wearing?" she asked.

I flashed my mom a thumbs-up sign. "I'm wearing jeans and my red hoodie."

"Okay, then I'll wear my fleece Polo pullover. See ya in a few minutes."

Mom came over and put her arm around me. "See? You were worried for no reason."

I shrugged her arm off and went to put my shoes on. Asia's parents were working out in the yard when we got there. Mr. Milanowski remembered my name. Asia got in the backseat with me and pulled out some magazines from her lilac backpack.

We got to Saugatuck and Mom gave me money to buy both Asia and me lunch with plenty left over for snacks and souvenirs. My mom was pretty generous when it came to giving me spending money. Asia and I went to the Saugatuck drugstore first because she said it had a soda fountain. We sat up at the counter and ordered sodas, hot dogs, and popcorn.

"Look at the guy sitting over there," she said. "He looks exactly like Jack Brogger."

He had Jack's five o'clock shadow and his signature sunglasses too. However, his skin wasn't as nice as Jack's. Jack had perfectly bronzed, smooth skin, but this guy had sunspots, a bit of acne, and he was a little blotchy. Then he moved his wrist to look at the check and my heart skipped. He had the same star tattoo on the inside of his wrist that Jack had. It was Jack. I elbowed Asia.

"What?" she asked.

I mouthed, "It's him," and she stared at me. I pointed to my wrist and said, "Check the tattoo."

Her eyes widened. Jack left, so we got up to pay. We raced outside, but he was gone. We tried looking for him, but we didn't see any sign of him anywhere, so we decided to shop and hoped we'd run into him. She found some cool flower bracelets and we both decided to get one. She bought a purple one for herself and I got one with all different colors. I decided to get a blue one for Simone and a red one for Charlotte.

"I really want to go find Jack," I said.

"I know, but look at these shimmer powders," she said, testing them on the back of her hand. "I'm getting these too. Okay, let's check out and then go look for him."

We both ended up buying shimmer powder, lip gloss, and vanilla candles. I'd never bought a candle before, but Asia said she loved them and they did smell like cake batter.

"This heart pillow would go with my Teen Couture bedroom stuff," she said. "Have you gone to the Maxi's store in Spring Lake?"

"No, why?"

"They had that stuff super marked down there. I would never have been able to get my comforter if it weren't on clearance. "

I nodded. All this time I thought Asia's family had a ton of money. She told me she and her mom loved to bargain hunt and go to outlet stores.

"You should come with us sometime. Morgan thinks it's lame, but my mom says why should you spend so much money on something just because of the name on the label?"

We went into a French-style store and she smelled all the lotions. She was telling me to smell her wrist when she stopped in the middle of her sentence.

"Jack walked past the store," Asia said, grabbing my arm.

We went outside and figured he must have gone into the bookstore. She knelt down, retying her shoe until he came out with a big bag. I almost fainted when he glanced over at us and nodded.

"He acknowledged our existence. So hot," she said. "Let's see where he goes."

He went into a modern furniture store and the owner took him upstairs. We would have followed him, but there was an "Employees Only" sign. We got bored waiting, so we decided to get some ice cream next door so we'd see him when he walked out. She ordered a scoop of espresso ice cream, so I got the same flavor. I had tried coffee once and didn't like it, but I didn't want to look like a kid in front of her. She paid for mine, which I thought was cool.

"He's so amazing," I said.

She nodded. "He's not as, I dunno, perfect-looking as he is in his videos though. I guess famous guys need makeup too."

I had never thought about celebrity guys wearing makeup, but it made sense. No wonder they all were so perfect in the magazines while real guys were never as flawless as the ones on TV.

"You know, Simone told me all the high schoolers on the TV shows weren't even teenagers. Some were like, in their thirties, which was why they were so sophisticated looking. She said the guy who played her brother was twenty-five, and he was playing a sophomore in high school," she said. "I'm still hungry. Do you want to get some pizza?"

Next Door To A Star

I would have liked to stay and wait for Jack, but it didn't look like he was coming down anytime soon.

"We could go to the New Hummingbird—I've seen other celebs go there, so maybe he'd stop by," she said.

"Good call. I did see they have a back room for special guests, so maybe we'd get a glimpse of him walking in or out."

We walked to the restaurant and she asked what I liked on my pizza. I hated green pepper and onion, but I didn't want to say anything. She suggested we get pepperoni, green pepper, and mushrooms.

"Okay, I can pick the pepper off—"

"If you don't like it then I'll only get it on half," she said.

The waitress took our order and I was worried we wouldn't have anything to talk about. She glanced around the restaurant and I tried to think of interesting stuff to say. I didn't know any gossip, so I asked her if there was anybody she liked.

"In our class?" She wrinkled her nose. "Well, after seeing Jack, there's no one else right now who can compare, but there's not a lot of guys at school to pick from anyway. I kinda like Wyatt Rogers. I mean, like, if the world was ending and I had to choose. What about you?"

I shrugged. I still liked Nick, and other than him and Jack, who else even interested me? I felt like I was being boring, so I tried asking her about Wyatt, but there wasn't a lot to say. I was afraid she was getting bored and going to tell Simone she had an awful time. I had to think quickly.

"You know, Charlotte thinks Will Fuller is cute," I said.

Asia's eyes got big. "Will's my cousin. Oh my gosh. He doesn't have a girlfriend right now, but he used to have a thing for Reagan. I can't believe Charlotte likes him," she said, stopping to take a drink of her soda. "I can't wait to ask him who he likes."

Oh crap. Charlotte would kill me if she knew I told anybody about her liking Will. She had sworn me to secrecy and I had ratted her out—to the guy's freakin' cousin no less. She was going to be furious...well, *if* she found out. I asked Asia not to say anything to Will or Charlotte and she nodded.

"I won't let him know she likes him, but it would be so cute if they got together. I didn't know Charlotte was even into the whole dating thing," she said. "I mean, not like I thought she was too young—it's...well... you know...never mind."

I hoped Charlotte wouldn't find out I told Asia about her liking Will, but Asia had promised not to say anything, so I figured it would be okay.

After lunch, we went back to the store Jack had been in, but the owner was downstairs now so we guessed he had left. We kept looking for him while we hung out the rest of the afternoon.

"I can't believe we saw him today," Asia said as she pulled her long, thick hair into a ponytail. "I'm so glad you saw his tattoo because I never would have realized it was him. Now I'm a little weirded out he wears so much makeup the rest of the time, but I guess it's okay 'cause he's such a hottie."

"Yeah, it threw me that he has...well, less than

perfect skin."

"Yeah, not to be mean, but his skin was pretty bad and his hair...it wasn't his finest day, you know? Normally, it's all perfect and instead, today, it was like, humidity wasn't his friend. He was still the hottest thing I've ever seen in my life though," she said.

"Without a doubt. Do you think he has a girlfriend?" I asked.

"I think I read in *Seventeen* that he's single now," she said, leaning forward. "You know, he went out with the girl in the *Starlight* video. She left her boyfriend for him, but they broke up after a few weeks."

I thought the girl in the *Starlight* video was the most beautiful model I had ever seen. She was one of those exotic types who look even better when they don't wear makeup.

"I can't believe Jack broke up with her. They looked so perfect together," I said.

"I know, she's gorgeous, but I read somewhere he said they had nothing in common," she said.

"Lies, they're both hot. They have that in common."

She cracked up. "I know, right? How is that not a foundation to build a lasting relationship? Anyway, I guess he meant they had nothing to talk about. It seems like they could talk about how beautiful they both are. You know, if he wears so much makeup on TV, then maybe she's not as natural and perfect-looking either."

I nodded. Somehow, even though we had seen how his skin wasn't perfect and he was way shorter than he seemed on TV, I liked him even more. He seemed more, I dunno, real or something, because he had blotchy skin. I guess before he had been too good to be true.

Chapter Twenty-Seven

Asia and I decided to wait and tell Charlotte and Simone about seeing Jack until lunch. I was dying to tell Char, but I held back. I gave Charlotte the bracelet I got for her in the morning though. She loved it and I thought it was nicer than the stupid shell ring Deidre got her, but I didn't point it out. Deidre had been hanging around Pilar a lot lately. It wasn't like Pilar wanted her around, it was that Morgan and Reagan had been acting like best friends and leaving her out. I guess even hanging out with your dorky cousin was better than being alone.

Simone had the bracelet I bought her on at lunch and Asia yelled at me to hurry up in the lunch line so we could tell them our news. I got my lunch as fast as I could and sat down to tell Char and Simone.

"Okay, so this weekend we saw Jack in Saugatuck," Asia said.

"Shut up. No way. You did not," Simone said.

"Yup," Asia said. "He even nodded at us—"

"Like a 'hey baby,' nod or a 'hey,' nod? Show me. Show me his *exact* nod," Simone said.

Asia got up and pretended to be Jack. Simone shrieked. "A total 'hey baby,' nod. You guys are so lucky. So what did he look like up close? Did he smell good? I bet he smelled good."

Asia nodded. "He smelled like the new Calvin Klein men's cologne."

"He seemed shorter than I thought he'd be," I said.

"Was he as cute in person or cuter?" Charlotte asked.

Asia and I exchanged a look. "Yes and no. He wasn't as perfect-looking as he is in his videos, but he was still super hot. His skin isn't flawless in person, and I dunno how to explain it, but it's like his imperfections made him even cuter," I said.

Simone suggested we all go out on Friday. We were talking about our plans for the weekend when Will Fuller came over to our table to ask Asia something. Asia's face got red and she shifted. Will shifted his glance between Charlotte and me as he grabbed some of Asia's fries. I had a sinking feeling he was trying to figure out which one of us liked him.

"Hey, I'm Will," he said, nodding to me.

"This is Hadley," Asia said. "She's new this year."

"I know, seen you around," he said smiling.

I didn't know what to do so I started picking the bits of shredded lettuce off my sandwich.

Charlotte spent the entire time staring at the back

of her juice box. Will probably thought she was such a dork since she couldn't even look at him. Poor Charlotte didn't even have a clue he knew she liked him. I felt so guilty. After spelling class, Asia grabbed my arm as we walked to my locker.

"I swear, I didn't tell him about Charlotte," she said. "I asked him if he liked anybody and he said he kinda liked Reagan, but he could tell I was holding something back. All I said was someone I knew thought he was cute, but I wouldn't tell him who it was."

"What a relief. I was so worried Charlotte would find out I told you. I can relax now," I said.

"Um, not quite. I guess Will kind of assumed it was you who likes him," she said.

"Well, as long as Char doesn't find out."

"Yeah, there's one little problem. He kinda likes you now," she said.

At first, I was thrilled a guy liked me, but then I thought about how Charlotte would kill me if she found out I had told Asia about her crush on Will. All I wanted to do was to find Charlotte and tell her a boy liked me. Only problem was she liked the guy. Why couldn't she like Max? Why did she have to pick somebody cute who now liked me?

"He asked me for your e-mail address. What should I do?" Asia asked. "I mean, I don't want to hurt Charlotte's feelings, but it would be cool to have my cousin going out with one of my friends."

I was so excited she called me her friend that I told her to give him my e-mail address. She gave me a quick hug and ran off to find him. I stood there in the hall wondering what I was going to say to

Charlotte. I should have been on top of the world. I mean, for the first time in my life I felt like I fit in somewhere. When I was a kid I used to have a Barbie coloring book, and it would show her at football games with her friends and hanging out with her boyfriend. Now I had a group of friends to hang out with, people to sit with at lunch, a best friend, plans for the weekend, and a cute guy liked me. It was everything I had ever wanted, but I felt sick because I was going to hurt my best friend when she found out I had given my e-mail address to the guy she liked.

"Hadley." Simone came running over. "I heard. Will's so cute. You're so lucky."

"I know, but Char—" I stopped when I remembered only Asia knew about Charlotte liking Will.

"This is so cool. You've got to come over when he messages you so we can read it together," she said.

Charlotte walked up. "Why are you going over there to check your e-mail?" she asked me. "I thought your dad hooked up your computer already."

I opened my mouth, but no words came out.

"Because Will Fuller asked for her e-mail address," Simone said.

Charlotte's eyes widened and she walked away. I tried to go after her, but it was like she disappeared into the crowd. Simone was right behind me and asked what Charlotte's problem was, but I shrugged. I didn't want to make it worse by telling another person about Charlotte liking Will.

"Come on. I want to stop and get a cherry cola slushie before we read Will's e-mail," Simone said.

I let her lead me to the ice cream parlor. She talked the whole way about how cool it would be if Will and I started going out and how she and Asia would have to find boyfriends so we could all hang out together.

"If you guys start dating then you'll be the only one of us who has a boyfriend," Simone said, playing with her straw.

Simone meant it as a compliment, but the thought made my stomach feel colder than the slushie. If I was the only one with a boyfriend, then I'd have to go places with him all by myself.. by myself with a boy. My stomach felt like it was the first day of school all over again. I was so not ready for this. My parents had never even brought up dating rules with me. I mean, I still slept with a teddy bear and kept my dollhouse around, so they probably never thought about me getting asked out. Plus, they didn't have a clue about Nick and me either.

"Let's stop at the newsstand. I want to see if they have the new *Teen Vogue*," Simone said, and I followed her out of the ice cream parlor.

I kept staring at our reflections in the store windows as we passed. Simone seemed so confident and beautiful in her gray and pink Juicy Couture hoodie. It must have been the way she carried herself, because I had almost the same outfit on—only less expensive—but I looked like a little kid next to her. Earlier, Aunt Faith told me I had seemed more sure of myself lately. I thought she meant because I had started wearing makeup, but she said it had nothing to do with cosmetics. She said confidence came from how you felt inside and what kind of person you were, and your appearance made no difference at all. And here I thought it was a load of crap adults said to unpopular kids.

We walked back to Simone's house and she checked my e-mail, but I didn't have any new messages.

"Can I braid your hair?" she asked. I nodded and she pulled my long hair into a ponytail and started making lots of little braids. It was more sophisticated than the ones Mom used to do for me.

"Have you ever had a boyfriend before?" Simone asked.

"No. I thought Nick was going to be my first. The guys at my old school were kind of immature," I said. I didn't add that all the boys there thought I was invisible, so there was never any hope of me having a boyfriend in Goodacre.

"I've had three real boyfriends. One was this guy, Chris, who dumped me the day I found out my parents were getting divorced. I called him crying and he was, like, 'Too bad, anyway, I don't think we should go out anymore. Maybe we could be friends.'" She pulled my hair tighter as she talked about Chris.

"Guys are such jerks sometimes," I said, thinking about the time this guy, Steve, from my old school, found a note I had written to Lexi and read it out loud on the playground. Then he played keep-away with it, and I made a fool of myself trying to get it back.

"Then Chris asked my friend Kasey to go with him two days later. I mean, he could have at least waited a week. It was so embarrassing," she said, pulling my hair so hard my head snapped back. "Oh, sorry."

I massaged my aching hair follicles as she went to check my e-mail again. She said I had a message from Will and asked if she could read it with me. I nodded and she almost twisted my arm off she was so excited.

Hi Hadley,

What's up? Did you watch the football game last Saturday? What's your favorite team? I like U of M in college football.

See ya,

Will

Oh, yeah. Real romantic. Still, I was relieved he wasn't asking me out or anything. If Will wanted to just be friends then it was fine with me.

"He's such a loser. I mean, asking you about football?" Simone rolled her eyes. "But he did write you on the same day he got your e-mail address. Means he likes you."

I wondered if some girls were given some sort of boy decoding handbook the rest of us didn't get. How could Simone tell Will liked me by him asking if I liked football? I had a lot to learn about guys. I was surprised he had e-mailed me at all. I mean, in the mornings I try to at least brush my hair after I wash it, but today I had barely gotten all the tangles out. I threw it up in a messy bun, and I didn't have any makeup on either. Most days I wore a little blush, gloss, and cover-up if I had any spots, but today I borrowed Charlotte's bubblegum flavored lip balm. I tried to look half decent most of the time, but on the one day I didn't try, I got asked for my e-mail address. Weird. I didn't understand guys.

"You can borrow my UM sweatshirt tomorrow," Simone said. "Then he'll think you guys have something in common."

Simone's sweatshirt smelled like her Bath and Body Works body spray. I loved it when she let me borrow her clothes because they always smelled so girly and nice. My clothes smelled like Snuggle fabric softener. Simone wanted me to e-mail him back, but I had no idea what to say. She decided to call Asia for advice.

"Will loves hiking and he's obsessed with anything to do with U of M. He also likes to watch anything sci-fi," Asia said.

He sounded perfect for Charlotte. She loved sci-fi, and hiking was her favorite thing to do. If Will liked *Charmed Lives* and Lance Cunningham, then I'd know he and Charlotte were meant to be—or they were fraternal twins separated at birth like Lance and his sister, Leocadia on the show. Well, they hadn't revealed the plot twist yet on the show, but Char's grandpa had read it on a soap opera spoilers website.

"I'm going to call him later and see what he says about you," Asia said. "Don't worry, I'll act like I haven't even talked to you."

I was nervous Asia would let him think I liked

him when I wasn't even sure how I felt. Simone could tell I was a little freaked out and she suggested we watch a movie and forget about guys for a while. She popped *Do or Die* in the DVD player and we sat on the sofa.

When I got home I wanted to call Charlotte, but I didn't know if she'd want to talk to me. Aunt Faith was over and she asked how school was going. I didn't mean to dump everything on her, but I told her about Will and Charlotte.

"Does Charlotte like him?" she asked.

"Yeah, I think he's the first guy she's ever liked," I said.

"But you like him too?" she asked.

I shrugged and said Will was cute, but I wasn't sure whether or not I liked him. I wanted to have a boyfriend—Nick. Nick was easy to talk to, sweet, thoughtful, and with another girl. That was over and I had to move on, but all I knew was I liked the fact Will liked me.

"Tell Charlotte you think Will's a nice guy, but your friendship with her is more important," she said.

"Sounds like something you'd see them saying on a rerun of *Duncan's Corner*," I said, making a face. "But if I do tell him that, then Will would wonder what my problem is and Asia might get mad at me."

I decided to call Charlotte after dinner. I was going to tell her I didn't try to take Will away from her. I had it all planned out in my mind. However, I freaked out when she answered and my prepared speech left me.

"I didn't like, go after Will or anything. He asked me for my e-mail address. I don't even know why," I said.

"Why didn't you tell me you liked him too?" she asked.

"Because I didn't—or, I don't. I dunno. I thought he was sort of cute. You know Jack Brogger's the only guy I like anyway," I said.

At least she laughed a little. "I don't have a chance with Will anyway," she said. "Actually, I had a crush on Nick too, but I knew I really didn't stand a chance there. Sheesh, you take all my leftovers."

She said it like a joke, but now I knew why she acted so weird whenever I talked about Nick.

"Char, I wish you told me about liking Nick before, but honestly, you and Will have lots of stuff in common. You both like to hike and watch sci-fi stuff."

"It's okay, you go out with him. I'll wait for Lance Cunningham to get sick of Madison and Chandler," she said. "Did you see today's show? Leocadia hinted she and Lance are related to Chandler and Madison's father. I think the truth might come out next week."

Asia called me later to tell me how her conversation with Will went.

"He said you seemed 'pretty cool' and he was hoping to hear from you," Asia said.

"I have no idea what to write in my e-mail to him."

"Just be yourself and tell him you're not into college football, but you watch other sports." Then she told me to ask him what kind of movies he liked. Seemed easy enough.

***

I set my alarm to wake me up a half-hour earlier to get ready for school. I curled my hair with Mom's curling iron and tried using an eyeliner pencil Simone let me borrow. I had to wash it off three times before I got it on semi-okay. Simone and Asia thought it was cute when I got to school, but Charlotte didn't say much. Simone had tried to get Charlotte to wear some lip gloss, but so far she had refused to put on anything more than Dr. Pepper Lipsmacker lip balm.

Asia had told me where Will's locker was and she wanted me to walk by and say "hi" to him. I didn't want to, but she and Simone said they'd go with me. We walked past him and I managed to squeak out a "hi." He had this weird look on his face when he answered me. I knew I shouldn't have tried to wear eyeliner. Maybe the boy-decoding handbook everybody else seemed to have also had a section on how to put on eye makeup.

Will didn't even come over to our table at lunch. Asia waved to him, but he waved back and stayed where he was.

"I don't get it. He told me he was excited you wrote him back and now he won't even come over here," she said.

"Maybe he's embarrassed because everybody knows he likes her," Charlotte said.

Asia shrugged. "I guess."

I was worried he changed his mind about me. I mean, I obviously tried to look better today too. I curled my hair and wore makeup. Maybe I didn't curl it right or something.

I ran into Nick after school while I was waiting for Charlotte. She had to stay after to work on a lab assignment since Deidre had messed up their experiment.

I almost never saw Nick at school because his classes were all on the other side of the building.

"So…how are your classes going?" he asked.

"Um, okay. Yours?"

"All right, I guess. Hold up, I need to stop by my locker here for a minute," he said. He opened it and I saw a picture of the new Tigers catcher taped to the back of the door.

"Nice picture," I said. "I like the new guy too."

"You seem a lot different today," he said.

"What do you mean?" I asked.

"I dunno. Different somehow. I'll see ya around," he said as he walked away.

Charlotte met me at her locker and asked what was wrong.

"I do not get boys at all," I said.

Chapter Twenty-Eight

The next day I didn't even bother to curl my hair. I put my hair in a braid, pulled on Simone's sweatshirt and went to class. Simone let me borrow her pink lip gloss because my lips felt dry.

"You're so lucky to have thick, dark lashes. You don't even need mascara," she said. "I have to glop it on before anyone notices I even have lashes."

I never wore mascara because it felt weird and was hard to get off. I did start curling my lashes recently because they stick out weird otherwise. Will waved to me in the hall and I gave a little smile. I didn't want to look overeager since he didn't seem interested in me anymore.

At lunch, Asia told us how she had a sneezing fit in the hall right in front of Wyatt Rogers.

"I always have allergies in the fall, but this was the worst. I almost sneezed on him," she said.

"I have bad allergies too," Charlotte said. "You should try using Angold allergy drops. They help me out."

Asia wrote the name inside her lavender binder. "Thanks, Char. Maybe it will help me keep my snot off Wyatt."

Will walked over and sat down next to Asia. "I like your shirt, Hadley," he said. I started to say it was Simone's shirt, but she kicked me under the table. Asia sneezed and her eyes got watery.

"I hate fall," she said, grabbing a handful of napkins.

"Well, I was gonna ask if you guys wanted to go outside, but I guess not," he said.

"Yeah, we've all got allergy problems," Simone said. "But Hadley doesn't. Why don't you guys go?"

I asked Charlotte to go along with us, but she picked up a napkin and pretended to blow her nose. She stuck her tongue out at me as I walked to the door with Will.

I thought I'd have nothing to say to him, but he was pretty easy to talk to. He asked what kind of music I liked and he made a face when I said, "Jack Brogger."

"He's okay, I guess. I kinda liked the song he did for the *Thunder and Steel* movie," he said.

"So do you like to read or…anything?" I asked, wondering if that sounded as lame coming out of my mouth as I thought it did.

He said was into the futuristic sci-fi series Charlotte loved. I mentioned I was going to ask my friend to let me borrow her books, but he told me he'd lend them to me.

"I probably don't have any books you'd be interested in," I said.

"Actually, I'd love to read the fantasy book I saw you with in the cafeteria the other day. The one with the dragon on the cover."

"Oh, that's Charlotte's. I've never read any of that series."

"Oh." We ran out of conversation and it seemed like the harder I tried to come up with something to say, the more my brain betrayed me. I couldn't come up with a single topic, but he didn't seem to mind.

Later, Simone asked me how everything went when I got to science class. I told her he was easy to talk to and she said the three of them watched us out of the cafeteria window.

"Charlotte said she thinks he's cute," she said.

"She did?" I asked, and Simone nodded.

After school, Will waited for me at my locker. "Want to walk home together?"

"As long as you don't mind if Charlotte comes with us. We always walk together," I said.

"No problem."

However, not only did he end up walking with us, but Nick was headed in the same direction, and it was super awkward with him alongside. Will and Charlotte talked the whole way about a movie they had both seen. The actor who played Lance Cunningham had been a mutant in it and Will thought he stunk in the film.

"Well, he's good on *Charmed Lives*," Charlotte said.

Will wrinkled his nose. "You watch that show?"

"We live for it," I said, and Charlotte nodded.

He shrugged. "Isn't Valerie Jackson on the

show? She's hot."

"It's *Valeria Joseph*," Charlotte said. "Do you know who Valeria is, Nick?"

"Yeah, but she's kinda fake-looking," Nick said.

His comment surprised me and I tripped—right in front of him. He put his hand out to steady me. Way to be graceful. Ugh.

"Well, this is me," he said. "Uh…see you guys later."

We dropped Charlotte off and went to my house. My mom was in the garden and we went inside to watch TV and have some grape juice. Will said Charlotte seemed pretty cool and I waited for him to say he liked her now, but he helped himself to a brownie. Valeria's new shampoo commercial came on and she whipped her head around so her blonde hair fanned out. She had on a ton of dark eye shadow, which made her eyes look all sexy and smoky.

"Nick's right, she is kind of fake," he said. "Like she's trying too hard."

"I don't think Valeria needs makeup at all, but I do," I said.

"Nah, you look better without it," he said.

My face got warm. Will left after we watched the video countdown show. My mom had a million questions about him when he was gone. I went over to Grandma's house to get away from her.

Simone was helping her mom rake leaves in the front yard and she called me over. I grabbed a garbage bag and helped her bag leaves.

"So, Will came over to watch TV at the house," I said.

She screamed and threw her arms around me. I dropped the leaf bag and her mom laughed at us.

"Aw, you guys are going out," Simone said.

I pointed out he hadn't asked me officially, but she waved her hand like it didn't matter. I told her what Nick and Will had both said about Valeria.

"Oh, I get it now—why Nick was acting so weird the other day. He made a comment that you seemed so down-to-earth when he first met you, but then he thought maybe he had read you wrong. I didn't know what he meant, but this explains it. I guess he doesn't like the whole overly girly-girl thing," she said. "Anyway, I called my Grandpa Hendrickson."

I asked her what happened and she said he wanted her to come out for a visit some weekend.

"Mom said I could go, so I think I might spend next weekend with him," she said.

Will messaged me later. He kept going on about some stupid show he watched about if aliens existed. It was the kind of thing that would have fascinated Charlotte, but I was bored.

***

The next day, Charlotte and Will talked about the alien show the whole way home.

"The guy from Roswell totally convinced me," Will said. "I mean, why else would the government need coffins tested to make sure they didn't leak?"

"Duh, who wants a leaky coffin?" Charlotte said.

"Um, you guys? Can we talk about something else?" I asked. "Something that doesn't involve bodily fluids oozing out of caskets?"

Will seemed like he forgot I was still there. I started talking about the U of M versus Michigan State football game going on Saturday. I thought it would get Will's attention, but things got worse because Charlotte knew a lot more about football than I realized. The two of them were off talking and I was left out—again. It seemed Will had way more in common with Charlotte, and it was getting on my nerves. I didn't mind if they got along, but if he was supposed to like me, then shouldn't he want to spend time with me? What was worse was the way Charlotte was looking at him. It was the same look Asia got on her face when she talked about Jack, or the look I got when I thought about Nick—except Charlotte had a much better chance with Will. I kept hoping it was my imagination and Will still liked me, but I had a bad feeling when Charlotte called me at night.

"Did you study for the math test?" I asked.

"No, I was busy chatting online," she said.

Maybe she was talking to Deidre, but I had bad vibes, so I asked who she was talking to online. She got quiet for a minute and then said, "Will."

I couldn't get mad since he technically wasn't my boyfriend and she had liked him first, but I wasn't thrilled.

"I didn't know you had his e-mail address," I said.

"I don't. He checked my profile online. It's no big deal. We talked about *Aliens Amongst Us*. Are you mad?"

How could I be? I pretty much stole the guy

from her. I told her I didn't mind, but I mentioned it later to Simone who thought it was a bad idea.

"If you like him then you're going to have to get interested in the alien crap he watches," she said. "Never let your boyfriends get too close to your friends. Look what happened with Pilar and me."

I thought Charlotte could be trusted, but then I realized she had trusted me not to tell anyone about her crush on Will and I had blabbed. She had also trusted me not to go after him and I had done that too. If there was anybody who couldn't be trusted then it was me. I decided to call Charlotte back and tell her I thought she and Will would make a better couple. It was obvious he liked her anyway.

"He's your boyfriend," Charlotte said.

"But he never technically asked me out," I said. "I know you still like him and I think you should go for it. And I know it's over, but to be honest, I still have feelings for Nick. Anyway, I'll walk home with Simone after school tomorrow so you two can talk alone."

***

Will didn't come near either one of us at lunch the next day. Charlotte hadn't said anything to me, but I knew something was up when she asked to borrow Simone's lip gloss. Simone's eyes almost fell out of her head as she passed Charlotte the tube. I couldn't say anything since I had encouraged her to go after him…only the second guy (other than Nick) who had ever paid any attention to me unless you counted the guy at my old school who threw gum in my hair.

I didn't even bother to wait for her after class. I went straight to my locker so I could avoid watching the two of them together. Simone came over to my locker and tried to make me feel better by telling me Will had crappy taste in shoes. Even Asia said he was kind of a loser and he always smelled like foot powder.

We walked outside and started to head to Scoops when I heard Charlotte calling after me. She was probably going to tell me he had asked her out—something he hadn't bothered to do with me. Her cheeks were flushed when she caught up to us. I didn't know if it was because she had been running or if Will had kissed her.

"Aren't you walking home with Will?" I asked.

She shook her head while she tried to catch her breath. "No, he waited for me, but I told him I had to meet you."

"Why?"

"Because I know you liked him and I wouldn't go behind your back," she said.

"I sorta did that to you."

She shrugged. "He's only some guy. I mean, he's fun to talk to, but whatever. And he said Lance was a bad actor. I could never like someone who didn't like Lance Cunningham. But um, I also ran into somebody else."

"Who?"

"Nick."

"Oh?"

"I asked him if he knew Morgan had lied about you having a boyfriend. He said Asia told him, but he wasn't sure what to think."

"Well, it doesn't matter," I said. "He's with Reagan now anyway."

"Yeah, well at least he knows the truth."

"Oh my gosh, I forgot to tell you guys what I read about Lance." Simone interrupted. "Valeria and the girl who plays Madison *both* used to like Lance and they got into a big fight over it at the studio. Madison almost got fired for pushing Valeria, but they worked it out and they're friends, and he's the one they're not speaking to."

I thought Valeria would have had better taste in men than to date Lance. It was one thing for Valeria's character, Chandler, to like Lance on the program, but for Valeria to like him in real life? He was too much of a player for her.

"Lance is dating the girl who plays his twin now," Asia said. "I saw it online."

"I'm glad they decided Lance wasn't worth ruining their friendship over," Charlotte said.

"Well, don't get upset, but Valeria caught him flirting with the makeup artist on the set, so she got mad and dumped his sorry butt," Simone said. "Char, I'll give you the magazine when I'm done because your grandpa will want to read it."

"Still, they didn't let Lance come between them," Char said. "Even if they only dumped him because he was a pig."

"Yeah, I mean, he's still cute, but he's no Jack Brogger," I said. "Of course, now I know that even Jack Brogger doesn't look like Jack Brogger."

"You guys, I have some news," Simone said. "I'm going to sign with a local agent. I won't be doing any TV shows from here obviously, but maybe I could do some commercials or whatever."

"That's awesome," I said.

"I miss acting, and I'd like to do some plays or something. I guess there's a theater around here I might be able to try out for, and Mom talked to the producers of my old show and they might write me back in for an episode where I come back from boarding school. It wouldn't be a permanent thing, but it would be fun to come back even if it was only for a day," Simone said.

When I got home, Will IM'd me and asked if I wanted to go to the movies with him and his parents this weekend. I'd never gone on a date before, and I had to admit I was kind of intrigued. Will was cool and it would have been nice to have a boyfriend, but Charlotte had already said she wouldn't ruin our friendship over a guy. I knew she wouldn't get mad at me if I went to the movies with him, but I didn't want to hurt her feelings or lead him on. Maybe nobody else would ask me out again, but I guess it would be okay if it meant I still had Charlotte as a best friend.

Sometimes it seemed like things were easier back when I didn't have friends and there weren't any guys interested in me, but I wouldn't trade my life now for anything—even if it meant I could be Jack Brogger's girlfriend...well, okay, maybe then, but I had next summer to work on it. By next summer, Simone might even be on TV again, and maybe she'd meet Jack. After all, he was always doing guest appearances on TV shows, so it could happen, and he and I had way more in common than he did with his video model. We both liked pizza, the color blue, and cookie dough ice cream. We were practically meant to be.

My phone rang then and I saw it was Nick. My heart jumped.

"Hello?" I said.

"Hey, it's Nick. Do you have a minute?" he asked.

"Sure."

"I heard about what went on with Morgan and Reagan and all that—um…stuff."

"Yeah?"

"I also heard you didn't have a boyfriend over the summer when we were, you know, talking."

"I didn't. Morgan made that whole thing up."

"Well, I wanted you to know that I believe you, and I'm sorry I didn't ask you about it right away," he said.

"No, I get it. I mean, you hardly knew me."

"Yeah, well, I should have asked. Anyway, I'm sorry about being so weird and about how Reagan was treating you. I guess she knew how much I liked you and kinda felt threatened by it."

"Seriously?"

"Yeah, we had a huge fight about it. She was telling me you did something and I defended you, and she was coming out with all sorts of crazy stuff—like that you were talking behind people's backs, and stuff I know you'd never do. Anyway, we broke up."

"Oh, well, I'm sorry if I caused problems between you guys," I said while crossing my fingers and silently asking for forgiveness for the giant lie I told.

"She was super jealous of you, and I started thinking about it—why am I with this girl who doesn't even seem like that nice of a person when the girl I really want to be with lives down the road?" I didn't say anything and he cleared his throat. "Um, do I have to clarify again that I'm talking about you?" he asked laughing.

"Very funny…actually, yeah. I do need it spelled out," I said.

"So…you want to hang out tonight? It's getting to be World Series time and we could watch the game tonight."

"I'd love to."

"Great," he said. "I'm mad at the whole situation for ruining our summer together. But maybe we can look forward to next summer, huh? Plus, basketball season is starting up soon. It'd be nice to watch the games together."

It was a strange feeling being able to think about what I'd be doing next summer with my friends—and now the possibility of having a boyfriend? The idea of planning stuff was exciting. In the past, vacations were only fun if Lexi was in town. If she was visiting family, then it was me sitting in front of the TV or reading a book. Now I knew I had a winter break to look forward to where I could go ice skating with my friends, and Nick was now talking about basketball season starting up soon.

"So do you want to watch over here or should I come over there?" he asked.

I remembered then that Grandpa had said he was looking forward to watching the playoffs with me.

"I usually watch the games with my grandpa—it's kind of our thing, but I'm sure he'd be cool with it if you came over. I'll text you to make sure it's fine. Is that okay?"

"Yeah, let me know what time."

I called Grandpa and asked him if Nick could come over.

"Now is this Nick the one you sort of like or the one who you get that dopey grin over when he messages you?" Grandpa asked.

"The second one."

"Ah, then you will need a chaperone. Okay, he can come, but I'm sitting between you two—kidding! Kidding!"

I texted Nick back.

Nick: Can't wait. ;)

I called Simone and told her the news.

"I'm so glad," she said. "He really is a sweetie and you guys are so cute together. I love how he blushes and gets so focused around you. He never does that with anyone else. I swear, Morgan made him nervous and even Reagan made him act all shy and weird. It's like he's more comfortable around you and can be himself."

"Yeah, I feel that way too. With Will it was so awkward."

Simone started talking about how we should save up and spend a weekend in Saugatuck next summer where maybe we'd run into Jack. I smiled as she went on about how we could check out his tour schedule to figure out the best dates. It was nice to be able to plan and look forward to stuff instead of trying to get through the day. But while Simone was already looking forward to summer, for the first time ever I was happy being where I was now. I had everything I wanted, and it was nice to sit back and appreciate it. Although I had to admit it was kind of amazing that Nick was already talking about us still being together next summer.

I got off the phone with Simone and walked over to Grandpa and Grandma's. I was about to go in when I saw Nick walking up. His whole face lit up as he smiled at me and I saw he had picked some wildflowers.

"For me?" I asked walking up to him.

He nodded. "There's something I have to tell you though. It could change everything."

I swallowed. "Okay, what's up?"

"I kind of lose it when the Tigers play badly, and I don't want you to dump me over that," he said, fighting a smile.

"Well, I guess I'd have to technically be your girlfriend if I was going to dump you."

"Hmm, that's true. I guess we better make that official so it'll be a little more difficult to walk away after you see me cry if they lose in the playoffs."

I smiled. "Seems fair."

"So it's official then?"

I nodded.

"Good, because I've missed you." He looked past me and then gave a little frown. "I can see your grandma watching through the curtains, so I won't kiss you, but know that I'm thinking about it."

"And I'm thinking about it back," I said smiling.

We walked into the house and sat down to watch the game. I went to help Grandpa bring some snacks in the room when I saw I had two texts. One was a pic from Simone saying she saw these cute necklaces online and wondered if Charlotte, Asia, and I might all want to get matching ones. I wrote back that I loved the idea and then saw the other message was from Nick. He sent three smiley faces giving smooches and said:

Nick: Look, I found a way around your grandma's watchful eyes.

Forget the best summer ever. I was having the best fall ever.

Acknowledgements

A big thank you to everyone who has supported me on this writing journey. My mom and dad, Justin, Amy, the Dennler family, the Slater family, the Tuesday Writers Group, the Cincy SCBWI group, the team at Limitless Publishing, Jennifer O'Neill, Jessica Gunhammer, Lori Whitwam, Rachel Whitwam, my Clean Reads family, and the teachers, profs, and everyone who inspired and helped me along the way: Dr. Zeff, Dr. Sarch, Mary Bostwick, Bob Houbeck, Dr. Charles Apple, Dr. Luis Mauricio Santos, Suzanne Verbruggen, Tom Wearing, Susan Shapiro, Nicky Schmidt, Diana Jenkins, Linda Grabowski, my amazing street team, and the authors for kids group.

About the Author

Krysten Lindsay Hager is an obsessive reader and has never met a bookstore she didn't like. She's worked as a journalist and humor essayist, and writes for teens, tweens, and adults. She is the author of the *Landry's True Colors Series* and her work has been featured in USA Today and named as Amazon's #1 Hot New Releases in Teen & Young Adult Values and Virtues Fiction and Amazon's #1 Hot New Releases in Children's Books on Values. She's originally from Michigan and has lived in South Dakota, Portugal, and southwestern Ohio. She received her master's degree from the University of Michigan-Flint.

Facebook:
https://www.facebook.com/KrystenLindsayHagerAuthor

Twitter:
https://twitter.com/KrystenLindsay

Google plus
https://plus.google.com/+KrystenLindsayHager

Website:
http://www.krystenlindsay.com/

Goodreads:
https://www.goodreads.com/author/show/8298036.Krysten_Lindsay_Hager

Instagram:
https://instagram.com/krystenlindsay/

Made in the USA
Middletown, DE
12 December 2015